# The Viking's

# Daughter

By

Marti Talbott

-

© All Rights Reserved

Editor: *Frankie Sutton*

NOTE: All of Marti Talbott's Books are suitable for young adults 14 and older. Sign up to be notified when new books are published at martitalbott.com

# CHAPTER 1

They had not a moment to lose.

With two gold coins, Karr Olney made a bargain with the queen's maid, and just before dawn, she lured the night watchman away from his post on the inlet shore of the Norwegian village. As soon as she and the guard were out of sight, and against the command of their king, seven Viking brothers held several full leather sacks above their heads, and silently waded into the water between two empty longships.

No one had ever stolen a longship.

The odds were heavily against them and if they got caught, the punishment would surely be death. Therefore, they chose the darkest night of the month and the time of morning that insured the blackness of night would barely begin to brighten.

Obbi, the youngest brother, set his sacks in the ship, grabbed hold of the port rim, hoisted himself up, and slipped inside. He quickly raised his head up and glanced around to see if he had been spotted. As near as he could tell, he had not. Cautiously relieved, he nodded to his brothers. More frightened than he had been in all his fourteen years, he continued to keep an eye out while he soundlessly relieved each brother of his belongings. Obbi crouched down, carefully positioned the supplies out of the way, and then received the food, their cloth wrapped weapons, shields, and two nearly empty water barrels. Finally, he received the bag that contained all of Anundi's wealth. At last, everything was onboard.

Taking extra care, the brothers stopped all their activity and allowed Obbi a chance to look for trouble a second time. So far, they managed not to make any noise at all, and he again gave the signal to continue.

To make certain they did not noticeably rock the ship, on opposite sides and at exactly the same moment, two more brothers raised their bodies over the rim, slipped in, and then ducked out of sight.

That left the four stoutest brothers in the water, and what they were about to do was the most dangerous part of all. They waded back out of the water and with their shoulders to the bow, the mighty Vikings strained to get the heavy ship moving. Their progress was painfully slow at first, but inch by inch, it began to move. The grinding noise the hull made against the dirt could not be helped, which made their labors that much more urgent.

At last, the ship was free of the land and began to drift away from the shore. Just as the other brothers had, two on each side of the ship, grabbed hold of the railing, pulled themselves over and crouched down.

Obbi kept his eyes peeled, certain they would not, and indeed, could not get away with it. Yet, so far, no one sounded the alarm and even the dogs had not begun to bark. That could soon change, but there was no time to worry about it now. The brothers took their assigned seats on the rowing benches, and when Obbi looked up, Karr, the eldest of the seven, was sitting in the stern holding the rudder handle. Karr clicked his tongue on the top of his mouth twice, which was the signal to begin, and Obbi knew just what to do. He should, they practiced it often enough.

One at a time, six brothers noiselessly lifted a long handled oar out of its storage place in the center of the ship, inserted them in the oar holes, and made ready to row. Too dark to see what he was doing, Obbi's oar knocked against the bottom of the oar hole. He caught his breath, as did they all, and waited, but still they were not discovered. More careful this time, he eased his oar into the proper place, got a firm grip, and waited for the signal.

In the scant light, Karr raised his arm in the air and then abruptly lowered it to begin the count. In unison, and just as they had practiced a thousand times, the brothers quietly set their oars in the calm water and began to row. Time and again, the men soundlessly raised their oars out of the water, slowly slipped them in, and pulled – until at last, they reached the mouth of the narrow and treacherous zigzagging fjord.

After months of studying the passageway, Karr knew exactly where each of the jagged rocks lay just beneath the surface of the water. Nevertheless, the sun was not yet giving off enough light between the steep opposing cliffs; he had never actually sailed before, and was not accustomed to gaging the agility of the rudder-steered longship. Just now, he could not be certain where anything was.

His heart beat wildly and he held his breath as they entered the darkness. He waited until he thought it was time, and turned the wooden, eight inch wide rudder just a little to the left. As if they too were uncertain, the brothers slowed their collective cadence – but it was not slow enough. The tip of a jagged rock scraped the shallow bottom of the ship and gave off a ghastly loud screech that echoed throughout the fjord.

They prayed first, that they would not sink, and second, that the villagers did not hear it. In any event, it was too late to turn back, so they each strengthened their resolve and kept going. Again, Karr held his breath and when he guessed it was time, turned the ship to the right. He imagined they would hit the side of a cliff, but they did not, and when his eyes finally adjusted to the darkness, he navigated them left and then right again. Mercifully, he could at last see the blessed light of early dawn shimmering across the open ocean.

Yet, they were far from being safely away.

Larger than most men, with the same blond hair and blue eyes as his brothers, Karr got up and knelt down to see if there was more water in the bottom of the ship than he could attribute to their boarding. It was still too dark to see clearly, but he decided if the jagged rock had caused a leak; it wasn't going to quickly sink them. Relieved, he stood up, returned to his seat, drew his sword, and began to tap a faster rowing cadence on the deck of the ship.

To make it across the incoming waves, they needed more speed, so he steadily quickened the cadence. Even though the shorter ship was built to carry only fifty men instead of the normal hundred the bigger ships carried, it was doubtful only six, no matter how stout, could actually succeed. Yet, they had to try.

The six rowing brothers gritted their teeth, ignored their aching arms and their sweat soaked bodies, and concentrated on the ever increasing cadence. At least now, they didn't have to worry about making noise when they lowered the oars, but the work was harder and exhaustion threatened to overtake them with each new pull of the oars.

They faced the waves head on and to their amazement, they broke through the first, the second, and each one after that until, at last, they were far enough out to set sail. Mercifully, Karr stopped beating his sword. His brothers lifted their oars out of the water, drew them in, and quickly stowed them in the bottom of the ship.

It was not yet time to rest.

They stuffed the wooden disks in the oar holes, unfolded the massive, thickly woven hemp sail, and hoisted it to the top of the mast. Next, they tied the thick bottom ropes to opposite sides of the ship, and with a loud pop, the wind snapped the sail taut. It soon caught the steady southeastern wind and the ship began to pick up speed.

Eager to get them quickly into a cloudbank, and with more vigor than he should have, Karr turned the rudder too far. The ship began to tilt, brothers began to slide to the side, and Obbi barely grabbed hold of the sail rope in time to keep from being tossed into the sea. As quickly as he could, Karr adjusted the rudder until the ship righted, wiped the sweat off his brow, and sailed them into the protection of the clouds.

Exhausted, the men got back to their seats and tried to calm their apprehensive heavy breathing. Even wrapped in the misty clouds, none of them were certain if their voices could still be heard, so they remained quiet for several long minutes.

Obbi was the first to speak up. Finally able to see more than just his brother's shadowy figure, he glared at Karr. "Next time, you row and I'll steer the ship."

"Gladly," Karr answered. He could not quite believe they had actually gotten away, nor that clouds waited to hide them as the wind carried them farther out to sea.

Hani could not believe it either. Born just ten months after Karr, Hani was pretty sure he knew what Karr was thinking. "Grandfather said he would watch us from above when we sailed. So far, he has kept his word," he said, as he tried to rub the cramp out of his left arm.

"He also said he would be in heaven to greet us," Obbi sneered, "and we nearly laid eye on him this very day."

Karr raised an eyebrow. "Was it not you who said I should command the ship?"

"'Tis doubtful," Obbi answered.

"Aye, 'twas him," Hani argued, "and we all agreed."

"Only because the lot of you dinna want to be the one to sink us," Karr reminded them. "If you have changed your minds, I shall hear about it now."

"Leave him be," Magnus said. "We are alive and I doubt any of us could have done better." It was no surprise that Magnus stood up for Karr, for he always did.

Steinn, the brother born between Hani and Magnus didn't care who did what. He was more interested in making sure there wasn't a hole in the bottom of the ship, and that all the oar hole disks were properly placed to keep the water out. There was another plugged hole in the ship, one which allowed them to release excess water when heavy rain threatened to sink them. It was next to that hole he would most often sit.

"Then you have not changed your minds?" Karr looked from brother to brother, saw each shake his head and then turned back to Obbi. "And you, brother, what say you?"

Obbi sighed. "I say we should all learn to steer, lest a sea monster swallows you up and the rest of us are lost forever."

"I agree," said Karr.

Obbi wrinkled his brow. "You do?"

"I do and we've plenty of time to…"

"Look," Nikolas interrupted. Born after Magnus, but before Almoor and Obbi, he pointed toward the shore. The fog was beginning to lift and in the distance, they could see the beautiful green landscape and the majestic snowcapped mountains of Norway.

"Take a good long look, lads," Hani whispered, "'tis the last we shall see of home."

Each was lost in his own thoughts and none of them spoke as the place of their birth, and the burial place of everyone they loved, slowly decreased in size. It was indeed a wondrous land once filled with love and laughter, but to stay meant living the kind of life Anundi lived – the kind he vowed his grandsons would never see. "See Scotland, laddie," Anundi said with his last breath. "See her, give her your pledge, and love her well."

Karr promised they would and he had been true to his vow, but he was worried. He remembered his grandfather's instructions well. He should, Anundi began teaching him when he was not yet eleven, and repeated everything again and again, until Karr could recite it in his sleep. They were away, just as Anundi said they would be, but did they bring enough provisions, would it rain often enough to fill their water barrels, and more importantly, would the Vikings give chase? He took a forgotten breath and turned the rudder until the rising sun was just above his right shoulder. It was a technique he would use often to keep them on a necessary southwesterly course.

With the wind lifting the ends of his long blond hair, the nearly seven foot giant with strikingly defined features, turned his thoughts to something far more desirable. He wanted a wife, and according to Anundi, the women of Scotland were more pleasing than most. He was not certain what kind of wife he wanted, but one thing was for sure – he dreamed of her often enough and he would know her when he saw her. His mind filled with thoughts of her, he looked out over the endless water with excited hope in his heart.

# CHAPTER 2

With so many siblings to care for, rare were the times Catrina MacGreagor could climb the hill of a morning, look down on her small Scottish village, and spend the precious moments of solicitude needed to contemplate the silent passing from childhood into womanhood. At fourteen, she was as tall as she would be, or so everyone said. The daughter of a Viking who found himself stranded in Scotland years before, her long hair was the same light blonde as her father's, and her soft blue eyes were normally filled with goodness and kindness. She wore the usual off-white, long wool dress tied at the waist with twine. Her sword and dagger strings were tied over the twine, and she wore a woven leather headband to keep the hair out of her eyes. Except for the normal fears of being attacked by a neighboring clan, or dying of a dreaded illness, hers was a good life filled with all the love a family and a close-knit clan had to give.

The village below was indeed small. Smoke rose from open cooking fires for those who had not yet built a hearth inside their cottages, the dogs and cats were beginning their usual hunt for food, the rooster crowed, and some of the men were already heading off to tend the animals. Spring promised new lambs, calves and colts to add to their small but necessary herds and flocks. Wild fruit trees would soon offer apples, pears, crabapples and plums, but what she loved most, was when the rhododendron buds opened and filled her world with glorious red and pink flowers.

All that should be enough to make any young woman deliriously happy. Yet, her desire for a different kind of love – the kind only a man could give her, seemed to be increasing daily. It was perplexing, and with no mother to guide her, she often knew not what to make of it. There were simple explanations from well-meaning others, rumors and things to giggle about with her best friend, Kenna, but her lack of clear understanding plagued her.

Therefore, she decided against taking a husband.

Even so, and although she knew not who or where he was, there were times when she could almost feel his arms around her. It was a fascinating kind of awareness she could not describe and dared not share – not even with Kenna. She could but wait, and while she waited, there were meals to prepare and chores to do, so Catrina once more gave up her precious quiet time and started back down the hill.

*

In a Viking ship made of iron and carved oak that curved upward in both the bow and the stern, the brothers shared their first meal at sea. So far, none of them suffered seasickness, all of them were warm enough in their heavy fur lined cloaks, and for the most part, they were enjoying the voyage.

To ward off fearsome sea monsters, the top of the bow had been shaped into the fierce head of a dragon, with its tail carved into the oak stern. Just in case that was not good enough, on each side of the ship was the golden image of a roaring lion. On the top of the solid oak mast that was positioned a little off center, a golden bird moved according to the direction of the wind. Obbi especially liked watching it change positions.

Three years older than Obbi, Nikolas couldn't wait to see if he could read the stars, and as the sun began to set, he made his bed and laid down to watch the yellow turn to blue, and then to the pitch black of night.

"Grandfather taught us well," said Hani as he wrapped up in his cloak and prepared to sleep sitting up with his back against the bow of the ship.

"Aye," was all Karr said. He still sat on the bench near the rudder and was known for carrying on long and involved conversations, but just now, they were facing their first night at sea, and he was anything but confident. So long as the wind did not change, he imagined they would do well, and tried not to make himself sick with worry.

"How many days did Grandfather say the voyage to Scotland would take?" Obbi asked.

"Speak the language of the Scots, brother," Karr charged. "We are Norsemen no more."

Obbi cleared his throat and did as he was told. "How many days?"

Karr nodded his approval. "A month, providing we dinna get lost."

"We shall not get lost," Hani said. "We have learned the placement of the stars, the moon and the sun. Fret not, brothers, for we shall soon see Scotland."

Steinn was normally the quiet one, not that he could get a word in edgewise when the seven of them were together, but he was certainly not afraid to speak out when he had something to say. "I am not so easily convinced. Knowing which way to sail is but a part of it. We face sea monsters, days when the sail will not catch the wind, and other days when the winds are harsh enough to throw us into the sea."

Hani shrugged. "We can but do as best we can."

"And if it dinna rain often enough to fill our water barrels?" Steinn asked. None of the brothers quickly answered, and he was not surprised.

"Brother," said Karr at length, "we all fear the same. We knew full well, for Grandfather warned us, yet we all agreed to come."

"I know," Steinn admitted. "'Tis that now 'tis real. We are here and I care not to watch a brother die."

"Nor do I," Karr agreed. "Yet, Grandfather said he dinna hear of Vikings dying for lack of water in the North Sea. I find comfort in that."

"He is right," said Hani, "I heard him say it as well. I would rather die from lack of water, than to sail with the Vikings. To that, did we all not agree? You've not changed your mind, have you?"

"Nay," Steinn answered. He puffed his cheeks and wrapped his cloak tighter around him before he settled down to sleep.

Of the seven brothers, the last three, Nikolas, Almoor, and Obbi were too young to remember their father and Karr was the best storyteller they'd ever heard. "Tell us again about Father," Almoor said.

Karr was expecting that to come up at least once or twice on the journey, but perhaps not this soon. Even so, it might help them relax and become tired enough to sleep. "Very well." He paused to gather his thoughts. "What I remember most is the way he loved our mother. He came home but once or twice a year, but as soon as his ship landed, he was the first to jump to shore and run to find her. When he did, he gathered her in his arms, repeatedly kissed her neck and wouldn't let go until she pounded his shoulders. Once, I saw him…"

"But," Almoor interrupted, "when the lads blew the goat horns, why did she not go to meet him?"

"She greatly feared the day he would not come home, and wished to be in the cottage when she got the unhappy news."

"He was a great fighter, and she need not fear he would die in the beginning," Hani added.

Karr nodded, although it was becoming too dark for the others to see him nod. "Aye, but that was before the King said Grandfather was too old to sail."

"What had that to do with it?" Nikolas asked.

"Grandfather was always there to protect his son. 'Tis one reason Grandfather dinna want us to sail with the Vikings...our father would not be there to protect us."

"Besides," Almoor teased, "Karr is too gentle to be a Viking fighter."

Karr rolled his eyes. "Grandfather also said that the search for riches is like a fever that cannae be cooled."

"Did Father have the fever?"

"Nay," Hani answered, "he wanted to be home with us, but he gave his pledge to the king."

"I remember running down the hill every day," Karr continued, "and sitting on the beach hoping to be the first to see the longships appear in the passageway. Every day I went without fail, and then one day, it happened."

"How many years were you?" Obbi asked.

"I was but ten years."

"And already he was the biggest laddie any had ever seen," Hani boasted. "The other laddies stayed well clear of him."

"I would too, were he not my brother," Obbi smirked.

"What happened then," Almoor asked.

Karr smiled. Almoor had heard the story countless times, but he always asked the same question – what happened the day their father did not come home. "Well, to be the first to spot a ship coming through the passageway was a dream come true. I stood up, shouted, jumped for joy, and danced a little jig…if you must know. The horn blowers soon sounded and I stayed not just to be the first to see father, but to count the ships."

"How many did they lose?"

"Three ships dinna return," Steinn answered. "I counted them too."

"But Father's ship did return," Nikolas said.

"Aye, his ship returned, but he was not on it." Karr paused, as he always did, trying not to relive the heartbreak he felt that day. "He died in the land of the Saxons, we later learned." At this point, he always hurried to finish the story just to get it over with. "Mother took to her bed, and that very night, Obbi was born. She gave him Father's name so we wouldn't forget him."

"Then she too died," Obbi softly muttered.

"Aye," Karr admitted. "She said her life left her the day he died. She lived another year before she gave up the ghost and went to be with him. Anundi dinna speak for nearly four days, but then he came to get us. He harshly took hold of my shoulders that very day, and made me vow never to sail with the Vikings."

"Aye, he did the same with all of us," Hani added, "even you, Obbi, though you were but a year old."

"And now we keep that vow," said Steinn. "I am comforted now. Grandfather would not have sent us if he feared we would die."

Nikolas went back to trying to read the stars. "Say again how we are to find the right village."

"'Tis two villages parted by a river," Karr answered.

"Suppose there are many villages parted by rivers?"

Karr answered, "Grandfather sailed the coast of Scotland countless times and saw no others."

"Grandfather dinna say how our arms would hurt from rowing either," Obbi complained.

"If you jump now, Obbi," said Hani, "you might reach land before you drown."

Obbi rolled his eyes. "I cannae, my arms are too tired to swim." He liked it when he could make his brothers smile, all save Hani, who never smiled, but he was not pleased when they were laughing at him.

"Something is amiss," said Nikolas. "The stars look just the same as they did last night on land."

"Sleep, brothers," Karr commanded. "I shall take the first watch." He stood up to stretch his legs, and waited until they settled down and went to sleep. His brothers did not always obey, but for the voyage, they vowed they would, and so far, he was well pleased with each of them. Being the eldest was never easy, and often were the times he wished he wasn't. Fortunately, he was the biggest too, at least so far. How big Obbi would get was anyone's guess. Already at six foot, six inches, he was still growing.

Their grandfather was a proud and mighty Viking, who told wondrous stories of landing on the shores of Scotland. Almoor was right – stealing, killing, and fighting, was not in the nature of Anundi's beloved grandsons. The brothers were not timid and not above fighting when necessary, but they did not relish the thrill of surviving a battle brought on by a Viking raid. Therefore, it was good that they escaped and even better that they managed to stay together.

Karr lifted his gaze to the billions of stars in the sky and whispered, "Thank you, Grandfather."

*

Of all the people Catrina knew, Ronan Macoran was the silliest and the most annoying. From the time she turned twelve, he began to come to the MacGreagor village and follow her around. That was before her father ran him off. After that, he took to hiding in the bushes where he could watch her, until her father gave her a sword. Everyone had to go to the bushes for their comfort from time to time, and Catrina wanted no part of him watching her. Therefore, she took to drawing her sword and shoved it into the nearby bushes. Twice, she nearly stabbed him. After that, he stayed much farther away.

This day, however, he was bold enough to stand up and face her.

"You again," Catrina sneered. "Have you no chores to do?"

"I am a hunter now," Ronan proudly answered.

His red hair seemed darker than the last time she had seen him up close. He had a funny sort of pointed beard that did nothing for the shape of his square jaw. His piercing green eyes had not changed, however, and she found nothing at all enticing in them. "I pity the animals. Do go away afore I am forced to call my father."

Even his grin struck her as silly, for only one side of his mouth curled upward. "I have chosen you, Catrina MacGreagor."

She stood her ground, put her hands on her hips and glared at him. "I dinna wish to be chosen. Be gone with you."

"I shall be the next Macoran laird, and then you shall be honored to be chosen by me."

"You? The next Macoran laird? That, I shall never see."

"You *shall* see it."

She narrowed her eyes even more. "I shall count to five and if you are not long gone, I shall scream."

He watched her serious eyes, decided she would truly do it, turned, and hurried back through the bushes. Ronan found his horse, quickly mounted, and rode away. The last thing he wanted was to have to fight the Viking, Stefan MacGreagor. He might actually have to someday, but not today.

"May you fall off your horse and break your neck, Ronan Macoran," Catrina scoffed. "The next Macoran laird, indeed."

*

The first two weeks in the longship were the hardest on the brothers. Used to a table heavy laden with all manner of foods Nikolas prepared for them, they were reduced to hard bread that would soon be unpalatable, vegetables that were wilted and rotting, and dried fish and meat. They were expecting it, but it didn't make it any easier when the time came.

Reading the stars was not as easy as they thought either, and occasionally the brothers argued about it. The voyage seemed hardest on Obbi, for he was still an active boy with no place to work off his energy. He tried rowing alone once, and managed to turn the ship slightly. He was proud of his accomplishment – the others were annoyed.

For the most part, all they saw was an ocean without end. They suffered sunburned skin, a lack of water until the first good rain filled their empty barrels, and daily dwindling rations. Overcast skies made it impossible to read the stars and left them in the darkest nights they had ever seen. Rain demanded they take down the sail and spread it over themselves for protection. The ship filled with water and without a sail, they drifted off course. Once the rain stopped, Steinn pulled the plug to let the water out, while the others used their helmets to toss the excess back in the ocean.

On two occasions during the third week, harsh rain and winds brought severe waves that mercilessly tossed the ship around, causing all of them to suffer seasickness. By then, they were no longer worried about having enough water, but they were once more off course. By the end of the forth week, even Karr was convinced they were lost. The next day was bright and sunny, the water was peaceful, and it looked as though they could again read the stars to see how far off course they were.

"Aye, but the shadow tells us true," said Steinn. Early on, he had taken over navigation, which meant keeping an eye on the shadow of a round disk that sat atop an iron peg imbedded in the floor of the ship – that is, when the sun was shining enough to produce a shadow. It was also his job to tell whoever was manning the rudder to move it this way or that, so the necessary corrections could be made. He was only guessing, of course. Anundi told them to sail southwest from the Norwegian coast to Scotland, but who knew if they were already too far south? The last thing they needed was to land on the coast of the Kingdom of York, where Vikings ruled.

In the last rays of sunlight and for the thousandth time, Obbi leaned over the side to see what was behind them. "Not a ship in sight," he proudly announced. "They shall not give chase." Just once, he hoped to know something they didn't already know. His chances were slim to none, for Karr knew everything.

"He is right," Hani confirmed after leaning out to look as well.

"He is wrong," said Almoor. "They lie in wait for us on the coast of Scotland."

"How would they know to lie in wait for us?" Magnus argued. "They must return home to learn we have fled, and then set sail to catch up to us."

"Aye, and they shall return home, tired and wanting their wives and children," said Hani. "Obbi is right, they shall not give chase."

Obbi's chest was beginning to swell and he looked to Karr for confirmation.

After several thoughtful moments, Karr gave it to him. "I agree, we are safely away. Nevertheless, they may yet be in our path. We know not where they sailed and we must be vigilant still."

"Well," said Obbi, his chest deflated, "I was right by half."

Seated behind Obbi while Magnus took the rudder, Karr ruffled his brother's hair, a thing Obbi sorely hated. He spun around and tried to lash out, but Karr grabbed his wrist.

"Not until we reach land, wee brother. Then I shall let you..." He was interrupted by an odd sound coming from beneath the water. It was like mournful singing, but not like any singing they had ever heard, and it was not coming from just one place in the ocean. He abruptly stood up and slowly turned to look in all directions.

There it was again.

Obbi's eyes were wider than they had ever been before, and his were not the only ones. "What is it?" he breathed, standing up beside his brother. The water was still smooth and gave no indication that anything was amiss.

"I know not," Karr whispered. He darted under the bottom of the sail, took giant strides to the back of the ship and relieved Magnus of the rudder handle. He was certain they were headed southwest, but turning due north or south, might save them from what were likely the sea monsters Anundi spoke of. He chose south, turned the ship, and prayed they could sail away in time.

Just then, and only a few yards from the ship, three colossal black and white fish jumped out of the water in unison. All seven brothers rushed to the side farthest from the monsters, and when the fish hit the water, it caused a wave that tipped the ship their direction. All seven were nearly tossed overboard. Not one of the gallant men escaped their trembling, even the mighty Karr, as they struggled to hang on until the ship once more leveled. In a panic, Karr sailed them north instead, a course he maintained for the better part of half the day before he turned them west again. It was the last they saw of the unbelievably large fish. Even so, sleep did not easily come to any of them after that.

"I fear the sea monsters more than the Vikings," Magnus admitted the next day. He hated showing his fear, but denying it would be worse, especially since his brothers were just as frightened. "Have we not heard of sea monsters lifting a ship completely out of the water, and then dumping all the lads overboard?"

Nikolas boasted, "I do not fear them. Magnus alone would fill the belly of the largest, and I would gladly toss out two more brothers."

Magnus shoved Nickolas' shoulder. "Me? They shall eat you first."

"What day is this?" Karr asked, hoping to change the subject.

"We are in our thirty-fifth day." Hani answered.

Karr nodded. "We should see land soon. Grandfather said when we see the seagulls – then we shall know we are close."

Instead of seagulls, the men spotted a school of dolphins with odd shaped noses. The dolphins followed in the wake of the ship, swam alongside, and occasionally jumped out of the water. The sight calmed their nerves and delighted them all.

"Can we not eat one?" Obbi asked.

"And cook it how?" Karr asked. He watched the dolphins until the fish tired of their game and disappeared.

"How easy they make swimming look," Nikolas muttered.

"How little it takes to entertain us," said Hani. "What I would give to see the skirt of a comely lass, swaying as she walks."

Incredulous, Steinn asked, "Is that *all* of her you wish to see?"

"Quiet brother," Hani cautioned, "for Obbi is not yet old enough to hear such things."

Obbi rolled his eyes. "I know all about the ways of lasses. Gerti told me."

"What…when you were five and saw our cousin unclothed?" Nikolas taunted. "Did you ask what was wrong with her? Did you wonder of her missing parts?"

Obbi narrowed his eyes. "I wager Gerti told me more than she told you. You likely dinna ask."

"I asked before you were even old enough to talk," Nikolas shot back.

"Asked what?" Obbi pressed.

Nikolas had to think about that for a moment. "The usual, I suppose."

Obbi grinned. "Ha, you dinna ask at all."

Karr nodded for Steinn to take over the rudder and sat down opposite Obbi. "What did Aunt Gerti tell you?"

Obbi was taken aback by his brother's question, for few were the times when he was even asked. "Well, she said I was to treat a lass like the jewel I favor most."

"Shine her?" Nikolas jeered.

"Nay, not shine her," Obbi disgustedly said. "I am to cherish her, take care she does not get lost and keep her out of harm's way, just as I would a diamond or a ruby."

Karr nodded. "Aye, she told me the same. We are also to see that we take a wife with her wits about her. If she be comely, so much the better, but a wise wife is most needed."

"Unless she resembles a hedgehog," Nikolas muttered.

"A lad who looks like you cannae be particular," Hani teased. "What other lass would have you?"

Obbi ignored his brother's bantering and deeply wrinkled his brow. "Karr, how are we to know if she has her wits about her?"

"The same way you discern if her laugh is pleasing – you talk to her," Karr answered.

"For how long?" Steinn asked.

"For the space between meals, at least," Almoor put in.

"Or less," said Magnus. "Once I see the lass I desire, I mean to marry her right away, the same as Father did."

"Aye," said Karr, "but Uncle married quickly and look what he got – a wife who caused him pain from morn till night. As for me, I shall know a lass at least a week before I decide."

"A week!" Magnus exclaimed. "You may want a wife with wits, but if you wait a week, she is likely to find you have lost yours."

Obbi did not see the humor in that remark. "Gerti said we are to talk to them, just as Karr says."

"About what?" three of the brothers asked at the same time.

Obbi shrugged. "I asked, but Uncle came home for the evening meal and she dinna answer."

"I could tell a lass about the stars," Nikolas said.

Hani heavily sighed. "I am certain she has already seen them."

Steinn checked the position of the sun and turned the rudder just a little. "So long as the soil is good and we can live in peace, choosing a wife shall be easy enough."

"If the Scots let us land," Almoor reminded them.

Karr nodded. "Aye, if the Scots let us land."

# CHAPTER 3

It didn't happen often, but when it did, a low, guttural sound invaded the hidden castle, and sent Catrina MacGreagor's youngest siblings scurrying to her bed on the second floor. All four of them piled on, got under her warm, animal skin blankets, and covered their ears.

"Brave warriors, one and all," she said, 'tis only the wind."

"Tis a dragon," six-year-old Garbhan claimed from under the blankets.

Catrina laughed, "'Tis a hole in the roof. Not in all my fourteen years have I seen a dragon."

Just one year older than Garbhan, Dughall uncovered his face, turned on his side, bent his elbow, and rested his head on his hand. "That dinna mean there aren't any."

"Well, if you see one, I shall slay it for you."

"Catrina could, too," said Garbhan, "she's the bravest of us all."

"She's just a lass," Aileen mocked. At five, Aileen would much rather play with her clay doll than slay dragons.

The last member to be born into Stefan MacGreagor's line of descendants, little Conan peeked his head out too. "I shall be strong when I am grown. Father said so."

"'Tis not enough to be strong, a lad must be brave as well," said Catrina. "He dare not let the wind frighten him."

"I was not truly frightened," Conan lied.

The first born son and the only child older than Catrina, Wallace had his mother's auburn hair, but the blue eyes of his father. From the second floor landing, he stuck his head through the arched doorway. "Know what day this is?"

All four of the little ones turned to look at him. "What?"

"'Tis laugardagur."

"Not again," Conan moaned.

"Aye, again," Wallace answered. "All Vikings bathe once a week on laugardagur. We are Vikings, are we not?"

Garbhan frowned. "Vikings by half, you mean. I choose to be a Scot. They dinna bathe at all."

"Where have you heard that?" Wallace asked.

Conan frowned too. "How do you know what day it is?"

"Father marks the days on his board."

"Oh."

"Some MacGreagor lads bathe every day," Wallace added. "Father is thinking we should too."

Conan's eyes widened. "Can you not talk him out of it?"

"When have we ever been able to talk Father out of anything? Get up. The Scottie had another litter this morning." Wallace turned to go, but before he left the room, he shouted. "You best get up! We've a long day ahead."

"Who made him the eldest?" Garbhan muttered after Wallace was gone.

Catrina sat up and tucked one side of her long, blonde hair behind her ear. "Father did. Wallace came first, then me, then Elalsaid, Niall, Carson, Beatan, Dughall, Garbhan, Aileen, and Conan. Mother said all of us were father's idea."

"His idea?" Carson asked, coming in to see what all the rest of them were doing. "What does that mean?"

"It means, Father wanted lots of lads and lasses so the clan will grow big and strong." Catrina answered. "We are far too small still."

"You mean so we can fight the Brodies?" Carson asked.

Catrina nodded. "That, and so we are never taken as slaves."

"Like Father?" Aileen asked.

"Aye, like Father."

Aileen stuck out her lower lip. "I dinna wish to be a slave."

Catrina hugged her little sister. "Nor shall you be."

"It could happen," said Dughall.

"Not for long. Father would never stop looking for us, and Scotland is not so big he cannae find us." She smiled at the relief on all their faces.

"Tell us Father's story again," Dughall asked.

"I shall, but not until after we bathe," said Catrina. "We best get up now?"

The little ones moaned and two of them scooted back under her blankets. "I am forced to tell Father, then," she said, throwing the covers back. Again, she smiled as they slipped out of bed and scrambled off to get dressed, all but Dughall, who needed a special hug and a kiss on the cheek before he willingly obeyed. The castle moaned a second time and she expected to see them rushing back, but her challenge had worked this time.

Catrina slid back down and covered herself while the warmth in her blanket remained. She was not fond of getting up either and lingered for a little while longer. The second floor was split into two chambers – the one on the opposite side of the stairs was for the older boys, and the one on her side was for the girls plus the two littlest boys. The stonewalls were bare and their feather stuffed mattresses on the floor were too thin, but someday, when time allowed, they would make thicker ones.

Since the death of their mother, her responsibilities had greatly increased and stuffing new mattresses was very low on her list of priorities. The feathers were carefully saved each time a chicken was killed, but it would be a long time before there was enough for everyone. Another day was at hand, and at length, she forced herself to stand up, put her frock on over her nightshirt and tie the length of twine around her waist. She yawned, put on her shoes, and tied the leather band around her head in the back. She watched Dughall and Garbhan disappear out the door, and then noticed Elalsaid was not stirring.

Catrina walked to her bed and knelt down. "Are ye dead yet?"

"Not yet," Elalsaid mumbled. "Must we always have mornings?"

"It would seem so." Catrina tugged until the sister closest to her age sat up. Then she left her bedside and went to help little Aileen with her frock. "What a fine knot you have made, sister."

Aileen hugged Catrina and beamed at the praise. At four, she always needed help tying the twine around her frock, but she was five now, and she had finally mastered it. "I'm hungry."

"Then we best find you something to eat." Catrina scowled at Elalsaid's lack of movement, took Aileen's hand, walked out the open doorway, and started down the stairs.

*

The three-story hidden castle was not truly hidden – not from the trained eye, that is. It was built out of the same stone as the cliff behind it, and had slots instead of large windows. From a distance, the castle looked like part of the cliff. The same way a flute made music, the slots were the source of the groans, although the original owners must not have understood that. The frightening noise was most likely the reason they vacated the castle in such a hurry, leaving behind all their belongings, including a long table, chairs, utensils and half eaten meals long since cleared away.

As always, Catrina's day began with making a huge kettle of oat porridge to fill their empty stomachs. The walls on the bottom floor were sparsely decorated with cloth drawings and scattered weapons, including a three-pronged spear with a burnt handle, and two Viking shields. Along the wall nearest the large hearth was a long board used for storing wooden cups and bowls, and preparing meals. Small leather sacks containing herbs and spices hung from nails driven into the mortar between the stones, and larger bowls, covered with cloths to keep the flies out, contained crushed wheat for making bread and oats for their morning meals. If they were very fortunate, they had cinnamon to sweeten the porridge, but such was not the case this morning.

"Why does Wallace eat first?" Carson asked.

"Because the oldest must work the longest," Catrina answered, setting one filled bowl in front of Wallace and the next in front of Niall. She quickly filled two more bowls, and when Elalsaid finally came down the stairs, she handed them to her sister to take to the table. At last, they were all eating and she had time to take a bite herself.

She faced a long day of work as well. Once the children were fed, the kettle and bowls needed cleaning, and vegetables needed to be cut up for the evening meal. After that, it would be time to bathe the children and then there were outside chores, such as carrying water and helping in the garden. It was spring finally, but there was a lot more to do in spring.

"Father needs me most," four-year-old Conan bragged. "He said so."

"He shall, once you have learned to dress properly," his older brother Beatan said. "You've your tunic on backward again."

Conan glanced down, realized it was true, and gave his brother a frustrated look. "Will you help me?"

"I cannae, I too must help Father this morning." Beatan got up, dropped his empty bowl in the wash bucket and followed Wallace and Niall out the door.

"Wait for me," Carson shouted.

"Carson," Catrina said, "take a meal to Father, for he got up too early this morning." She quickly filled a bowl, remembered to add a spoon, gave it to her brother, and then watched him hurry off to catch up with the other boys.

Dughall had his elbow on the table, resting the side of his head in his hand while he ate. "Why must Father work so hard?"

Catrina patted the top of his head. "He greatly fears we shall not have enough to eat come winter."

"Oh."

Each morning was exactly the same. The boys hurried off, leaving the two oldest sisters to tend the four little ones, none of whom could quite grasp the concept of eating faster. Elalsaid wasn't doing much better. She was going through that dreadful time when thirteen-year-olds were slow, clumsy, lazy, and normally off in some far away dreamland.

Catrina sighed and decided to sit at the table herself for once. Her comfort only lasted until Conan finished eating and went to her for help with his tunic. Then Garbhan needed help with his shoes, Aileen realized she didn't have her doll, caught her breath and darted back up the stairs, and Elalsaid was not likely to move, even if the roof completely caved in.

*

Catrina smiled at the faint knock on the door and watched her best friend enter, just as she did every morning. With only three siblings to care for and a mother who did the lion's share of the work, Kenna MacGreagor was always finished with her chores long before Catrina was.

"You are early this morning," said Catrina. She shooed the youngsters out the door, including Elalsaid, and closed it behind them.

Kenna sat down at the table, sighed and wistfully looked up at the ceiling. "Is Grant not the most handsome lad of all?" A beauty in her own right, she had the red hair of her

Macoran parents, William and Andrina, who came to live with the MacGreagors soon after Stefan established the clan. She too, wore the simple frock all women wore, which was made of wool that was a bit scratchy sometimes.

"Aye, today at least. Yesterday, you favored Garth, and the day before, it was Donahue. I cannae wait until the day you fancy Ronan Macoran."

"Ronan? Catrina, how can you say that? You know I despise him. He is always hiding in the bushes so he may watch us. He thinks himself a great warrior and he does not bathe nearly as often as he should. I made mention of it too."

Catrina giggled. "Did you? How grateful we all are. I believe he has taken it to heart, for I cannae smell him lately."

"He is there nevertheless. He fancies you. He told me so."

"Well, I dinna fancy him at all. He is..."

"Silly?"

"Aye," Catrina agreed. "He looks at me differently than other lads."

"'Tis lust, my mother said."

"Is it? Whatever it is, I find it unsettling and I pity the lass who marries him."

"As do I." Kenna had a habit of twirling a lock of her red hair with her fingertips until it was tight, straightening it out, and begin her twisting again. "I would favor Wallace if he were old enough to marry. Father says he is not. How is it we are blessed with only three lads old enough to marry?"

Catrina opened a cloth sack on the shelf, reached in, and withdrew a wilted head of cabbage. She carefully examined it, removed the outer leaves and took the rest to the table. "You know how. We began with only seventeen husbands and wives and gained twenty-four more from the Limonds and the Macorans. Six lads and two lasses died, and only three marrieds already had sons. If it were not so, Wallace would be the eldest, and then what would we do for husbands?"

"But could they not have kept from having so many daughters? We are the eldest of eleven lasses, and for all we know, the three wait for the others to come of age."

"In that case, we must keep the lassies from coming of age…somehow." Catrina withdrew her dagger and began to cut the cabbage into wedges.

"Indeed we must," Kenna sighed. "We could choose a husband from the Macorans or the Limonds, if Laird Limond would let us."

"Laird Limond would let us, but our fathers would not. They wish us to stay here and grow the clan."

"Then Grant, Donahue, and Garth, are our only hope. Grant smiled at me this morning."

Catrina rolled her eyes. "Grant smiles at you every morning."

"I know, but what does it mean? He dinna ask for me yet, we must choose husbands soon, and how can we choose if they dinna ask for us?"

"In your case, 'tis a good thing none of them have, for you are too easily persuaded."

"I suppose 'tis true. I never can say which I favor most."

Next, Catrina retrieved several white carrots that looked edible, and began to cut them up. To those, she hoped to add beets, onions, salted meat, and garlic wedges for flavor. It all depended on what remained in the root cellar where the harvest was kept through winter. In spring, there was little left of the apples, plumbs, and wild pears, but soon the forest would provide strawberries and raspberries. She couldn't wait.

Catrina stopped her cutting for a few moments, and then thoughtfully said, "I see no need to marry until I am at least nineteen years."

"Nineteen? You have gone daft?"

"I have done nothing but care for children all my life. Surely, a year or two without little ones would do no harm. Conan is almost five, and in five or perhaps ten years more, he shall be well able to care for himself."

Kenna giggled. "Is he not intending to be the greatest of all MacGreagor warriors?"

"Aye, and someday, when he is twenty or thirty years, he may no longer fear as little as a howling wind."

Again, Kenna giggled. She withdrew her dagger and began to help with the carrots. "Why do the lads have stockings sewed to their long pants to keep their feet warm and we do not?"

"You wish to wear long pants?"

"Nay, I wish warm feet in winter with stockings that do not slide down constantly."

Catrina lifted her nose in the air. "I shall speak to my father about it, and if there is a way, we shall sew stockings to the hems of our skirts."

"Never mind, we would look even more unkempt than we do now."

"We look unkempt?"

"Of course we do, we are all in need of new clothes. And another thing, Macoran lasses wear linen under their skirts and we do not."

There were more carrots to cut up, so Catrina brought those to the table as well. "We cannae afford linen. We cannae afford anything but food, tools, and weapons."

"I know, but we can dream of it. I should like very much to wear linen on my wedding day."

"You think to marry in spring?"

"Aye, spring is the best time to marry."

"Why? Why is spring the best time? Is that not when the hardest work begins?"

Kenna lowered her brows. "I had not thought of that."

"I wish to marry in autumn, but not for six or seven more autumns."

"So you have said. I wager you shall marry before the year is out."

"Do you? And what have you to wager?"

Kenna considered that, while she sliced a carrot into three parts. "Well, if I win, you must regard me as a Queen of Scots for a whole day, and fulfill my every wish."

"And if I win?"

"You'll not win, but if you do…I shall cook all day for your family instead of mine."

"All day? Now *that* is a tempting wager."

"Done then. Do not get your hopes up, Catrina MacGreagor, for I shall surely win."

"'Tis where you are mistaken. I do not prefer Grant, Donahue, or Garth. Therefore, I must wait until some poor lad loses his direction, stumbles into our village, finds me vastly pleasing, and steals my heart away."

"If Muriel doesn't trick him into marrying her first."

When Catrina cut the next carrot, half of it shot down the table. She leaned forward, grabbed it, and put it back in the pile. "I have yet to see Muriel trick a lad and if 'tis her way, 'tis not working. She has yet to catch a husband. 'Tis a good thing too. We need Muriel to tell us what is happening in Clan Macoran. If she marries, she shall have wee bairn to care for and…"

"She only brings the news so she may come to see Grant," Kenna scoffed, "and when she has no news, she pretends to water her cows at the edge of our loch. She hopes he will come to her and sometime he does. 'Tis why I cannae abide her."

"Because he may prefer her over you?"

"Catrina, we have too few to let Muriel marry even one of our lads, no matter which one."

"Still, Grant does not ask for her either. I think he waits for you."

Kenna wrinkled her brow. "I wonder why he does not ask for me then. He seems attentive, but he does not seek me out." When she heard her mother calling, Kenna crossed her eyes. "I best go." She scooped up the cut carrots, dumped them in the kettle, wiped her hands on her skirt, and scurried out the door.

And so it was, that Catrina's day had begun just the way it always did – routine and boring, with too much to do, little ones constantly needing attention, and no time at all to dream of the man she would someday marry. She was right, she rarely went anywhere and if she were to marry a man other than the three in her clan, he truly would have to stumble onto the place.

*

A long, wide loch in front of the castle's courtyard provided ample water and fish, when the MacGreagors were lucky enough to catch them. More often than not, fishing was done at night when the men could lure the fish closer to shore with the light of a torch, and then stab them with their spears. Their cottages were situated on cleared land that stretched around the eastern side of the loch. In summer, they tended the crops and in winter, they built more cottages in preparation for weddings soon to come. As well, they began to build a high stonewall on the western side of the loch, to protect them from the fearsome Brodies.

Although the air was still a bit brisk, it carried the sweet scent of early blooming wild flowers. A Mallard duck brought her chicks to swim in the loch, the trees and bushes exhibited their new growth in bright green leaves, and each in the new litter of puppies were adorable. Their flocks and herds were not likely to grow large, for often they traded livestock for the wheat and oats needed to see them through winter. Still, keeping the cows and sheep out of the vegetable garden was a fulltime job for some of the younger boys.

Chickens pecked at the morsels of food on the ground, and dogs were allowed to do whatever they wanted, so long as they did not try to eat the chickens or their eggs. Instead, the dogs were counted on to keep the red foxes and the gray wolves away. None of the dogs were partial to any one family, but all of them were good at sounding the alarm in case of strangers or the more ferocious animals. All except old blue, a Scottie with bluish fur that had enough trouble just keeping one eye open long enough to eat the scraps of food the clan saved just for him.

The garden was situated alongside the castle, on the gradual slope of the hill. When it did not rain, which was seldom, the men carried buckets of water to the top and let it roll down the hill. When it came to keeping birds away, the cats were happy to help, and the dogs lay in wait for any rabbit brave enough to approach the cabbage patch. Yet, the garden, necessary to their survival, was a great deal of work. Rain the day before helped and on this day, all the men laid their other chores aside to help turn the wet ground and prepare it for the planting.

As all clans did, Stefan hung a shield from the branch of a tree and fashioned a rod with a sheepskin knob on one end. It was used to sound the alarm in case of fire or worse – a Brodie attack. It was also used to announce special events such as births or deaths. While not all clans got along, the number of times the shield was rung was a code, which meant the same to all of them.

The men normally bathed at night in a distant part of the loch, while the women bathed closer to the cottages, but the children were bathed in the daytime when it was warmer. Some of the MacGreagor little ones loved the water, but that didn't include two of Catrina's brothers. Every bathing day, Wallace and Niall had to forcibly strip them of their clothes and carry them into the water, which meant they got as wet as the little ones did. Still, bathing in the warm water loch each week didn't take nearly as much time as dressing them again.

As promised, Catrina sat on a log, dried little Conan's hair and got him dressed, while she began the story. "We must all know the story well, so we can warn our children and they can warn their children. Agreed?"

"Aye," said some, while others only nodded. There were shoes to put on, belts and twine to tie, and more hair to dry, with the eldest helping the younger ones.

"Father is the son of Donar," she began, "who was a mighty commander of seven Viking ships when they sailed the North Sea. Even before they left the fjord in their homeland, Father had a foreboding."

"What's a foreboding?" Carson asked.

"'Tis a feeling that comes over us when something is amiss. Father somehow knew he would never see his homeland again," Wallace answered.

"Oh."

"Donar named his ship the *Sja Vinna,* and when father was old enough, he was allowed to sail with them for the very first time. The other Vikings came to Scotland to steal what they could, but..."

"But," twelve-year-old Niall interrupted. His voice was changing, and it screeched, but he was getting used to that, "there came a great battle with our grandfather, Laird Macoran." Niall was growing so fast, it was nearly impossible to keep him in the long pants Wallace handed down. Just now, they were already two inches too short, not to mention wet from bathing his brothers.

"Aye, but as big and as strong as he was," Catrina continued, "Donar died that day, as did several other Vikings. The rest ran back to their ships and sailed away, leaving Father all alone in Scotland."

"His foreboding was right," Wallace added. "But Grandfather Macoran is a good and kind lad, who burned the *Sja Vinna* and gave Donar an honorable Viking burial at sea."

"And then Father married Mother," Beatan added. At ten, he wasn't old enough to bathe with the men, but he sorely resented still being considered a child.

Catrina nodded. "Aye, but not for a time yet. First, he was captured by the Brodies and made a slave. For three years, Father was in bondage, but then Laird Limond set the slaves free."

"And the slaves then made Father their laird," Wallace volunteered.

"You have heard this story?" a bewildered Conan asked.

Wallace tied the youngest child's damp hair back with twine. "Many times, as will you before you are grown."

"And then, what did they do?" Carson asked.

"Well," Catrina answered, "in slavery they learned how to build with rocks and mortar, and they built the cottages you see behind us."

"And then he married Mother?" Beaton asked.

Catrina turned Garbhan around so she could tie his hair back. "Aye."

"Mother passed," little Garbhan said. He didn't mean to, but he made all of them bow their heads in sorrow.

"Garbhan, we are all well aware of that." Catrina checked to see that all of them had their shoes on and then stood up. "Come, there is much work to be done this day."

"Is there not always?" Dughall muttered.

"We could pray for rain again," Conan suggested, taking his big sister's hand.

Elalsaid looked up at the clear blue sky. "I dinna think it will work this time."

# CHAPTER 4

While all ten children born to Stefan and Kannak MacGreagor had light hair at birth, some of their hair began to change to red and then to the auburn color of their mother. After each bathing, they stood in front of the castle, in stair step fashion and waited for their father's inspection.

He stood six feet, six inches tall, had long blond hair which he wore tied in the back the way most men did, and there was love in his blue eyes for each of them. He smiled and as he always did, he greeted each by name, "Wallace, you shall soon be as tall as me. Catrina, you become more bonnie each day. Tis time you choose a husband."

"What?" She eyed her father's sudden frown, bowed her head and shifted her eyes from side to side. "Aye, Father."

Stefan gently touched the cheek of his next eldest daughter, "Elalsaid, you are thirteen years and must soon consider a husband as well…but not just yet."

Elalsaid breathed a sigh of relief. "Thank you, Father."

"When may I take a wife?" Niall asked.

Stefan smiled at his twelve-year-old. "When you can work as well as any lad, then you shall be ready to marry."

"I don't want a wife," Beatan pouted.

"Nor do I," said Carson.

Stefan eyed their smudged faces. "And you shall not have one until you have learned to wash better."

Carson's eyes brightened. "If that be the case, I shall not wash ever again."

Stefan chuckled. "You will change your mind. And while I am reminded, Beatan, come next laugardagur day, you shall bathe with me."

Nothing could have made the ten-year-old happier and his eyes danced with delight. "Thank you, Father."

"Must I take a husband, Father?" Aileen asked, holding her clay doll haphazardly under her arm.

"Not if you intend to hold your wee bairn thusly so." Stefan rescued the doll and held it upright against her chest until she wrapped her arm around it. He knelt down and gathered her and his youngest son in his arms. "Who might you be?" he asked Conan.

"I am Conan, Father, do you not remember me?"

"Aye, but you were much smaller the last I saw of you. You have grown..." At the sound of a gong in the distance,

Stefan abruptly set the children down, stood up and looked toward the land of the Macorans. He listened, as everyone in the clan did, and counted the gongs. Unhappily, they stopped after three.

"Three times they beat their shield, Father," Wallace whispered. "'Tis…"

"Dinna say it, Son, we need not upset the wee ones." Stefan watched as the other clansmen began to come toward him. "Catrina, take them inside."

She did as she was told, although once they were inside the castle, she stayed outside to see what was happening. She watched as her father raised a hand, pointed at William, his second in command, and then pointed toward the Macoran village.

William nodded, whistled for his horse and as soon as it came to him, he mounted and rode around the edge of the loch. A few moments later, he disappeared down the path that led to the Macoran village.

Even then, Stefan waited until all the men were gathered before he spoke, "I fear Laird Macoran has finally passed. Arm yourselves, gather your families and take them inside the keep. We know not what the Brodies will do, but they can guess what has happened, the same as we. Wallace, climb the wall and watch, but stay hidden behind the branches of the tree."

*

"Aye, Father," Wallace said.

Catrina watched her brother race for the wall. It was almost forty feet long, and as tall as he, so he grabbed a low hanging branch, swung his body up and crouched on top of the two foot width. She had done the same several times and was well aware that Wallace could barely see the top of Laird Brodie's Keep. Yet, the rising smoke from the village hearths made its location clear. For years, they had watched the smoke rise in the distance, but rarely had they seen a Brodie up close. For the Brodies to attack the MacGreagors, they would have to fight the Macorans and the Limonds as well, and so far, the Brodies had kept their distance. Hopefully, that was not about to change. It all depended on who the new Macoran laird would be – and if he made an alliance with the MacGreagors, or gave his loyalty to the dangerous and terrible Brodies. Catrina only knew one thing for sure. They could trust Wallace to spot movement on the path that led to the Brodie village, and shout a warning at the earliest possible moment.

In keeping with what they had practiced, Catrina held the door to the castle open for the other women and children. Kenna looked especially terrified as she hurried past, and ushered her siblings to the place her mother thought was the safest near the center staircase. There was no time to consider the loss of her grandfather, although Catrina's heart was already heavy. Instead, she feared what they all feared – a violent Brodie attack.

Even then, she did not go inside.

She watched the men and the older boys run into the woods to take up their hiding places. Each of the children over twelve knew how, and could shoot a bow and arrow, but hitting the right target was sometimes questionable. Satisfied that all was going according to what they had practiced, her father took his place beside four other men in front of the castle, checked the position of his weapons, and waited.

It was idle time, time they could not spare, but such was the nature of a possible attack. Just before she went back inside, she saw her father glance at his eldest son, and then look toward the Macoran path to see what news William would bring back. The Macoran village was not that far away, but it was not that close either, so Catrina expected it to take a while.

*

She closed the door and dropped the long wooden bolt into place. She made all of her siblings sit on the floor and then raced up the stairs to the slot in the wall that faced the loch. She scooted a trunk closer, climbed up, and then peeked out. Grant MacGreagor stood not far from where her brother was stationed on the wall, and he did not look the least bit frightened. It made her ashamed of the nervous knots in her stomach. She had trained to fight from the age of twelve, but she never truly considered what a war would be like. Even now, she could not imagine it.

The passing of time seemed excruciatingly slow as they waited, and eventually her thoughts drifted to what her father said – it was time to take a husband. If Stefan insisted, she would choose Grant. There was something in the way he smiled that warmed her heart, yet Grant had never once shown a particular interest in her. Instead, he seemed to pay his attentions to either Kenna or Muriel Macoran. Perhaps he was no better at choosing a wife than Kenna was at choosing a husband. He was a stout man at nineteen, kind, cautious, and often funny, but if he wanted a wife, he had not yet said. She would have heard if he did. Indeed, if she must choose, she would choose Grant– if he would choose her. Yet, his arms were not the arms she dreamed of, and what could be worse than to pledge herself to the wrong man? No, she would not marry so soon – if by some miracle she could talk her father out of it.

She moved to a different slot in the castle wall, and when she did, she spotted movement on the Macoran path. It was far too soon for William to return, but there he was anyway, and another man was with him. The two halted in front of Stefan and dismounted.

"Laird Macoran passed in his sleep," said Alton. It was right that Alton Macoran had come, for he and Stefan had been good friends for years. Alton was Muriel's father, worked the Macoran land nearest the MacGreagors, and was often the source of important news. Occasionally, the news included a Viking raid on the villages nearest the ocean. As was the custom, anything that happened was passed from farmer to farmer and then on to the other nearby clans. Hunters also played an important role in the passing of information, but the most reliable news came from the farmers who were usually home all day to hear it.

At the passing of his father-in-law, Stefan hung his head in sorrow. "We suspected as much. How have you managed to get the word so quickly?"

"He passed early this morning. Everyone was so upset, none remembered to pound the shield."

"I see. He was the best of lads," said Stefan. "He shall be sorely missed."

"'Tis worse than that," William added. "Ronan has declared himself Laird."

Stefan's mouth dropped. "Ronan? What do the people say?"

"They are not surprised," said Alton. "He is a braggart whom most cannae abide. Still, he is the first to declare and must be dealt with first."

"Surely there are others," Stefan said.

Alton nodded. "Aye, but they have vowed not to fight until after we bury Laird Macoran tomorrow next."

"Has a rider gone to find the priest?"

"Aye, the priest lodges with the Limonds these days, and a lad has been sent to notify him."

"Is the clan in need of anything?" Stefan asked.

"Aye," said Alton, "we are in need of a laird with wits, of which Ronan has none." Alton glanced in the direction of his farm. "I best get back. One of our cows is calving and I am needed at home."

Catrina watched until Alton Macoran rode away, got down off the box, and then hurried downstairs. Soon after he opened the door, Stefan gathered his children and gave them the awful news. They took it bravely, but what else could they do? They were still expecting the Brodies to attack, and the room was filled with women and children who were near panicked. There would be time to mourn later. After their father went back outside, the little ones returned to their seats on the floor.

Catrina folded her arms, leaned against the wall and bowed her head. For months, they had dreaded this day and it had finally arrived. She didn't cry either, but she wanted to. All she could do was wait just like everyone else. Thankfully, the gong did not sound the attack, and after a time, when it appeared the Brodies were not coming, everyone went back to their daily chores.

Even so, Wallace kept his post atop the wall and watched.

*

During the evening meal, the castle was uncommonly quiet. The children knew death well already, and although

Laird Macoran had been too ill of late to see them often, they remembered him as a kind and gentle grandfather. Their father said hardly a word, ate his meal and then went back outside to work. Of the children, Dughall took it the worst. With sadness in his eyes, he stayed close to Catrina as she cleaned up, even getting in the way at times. At last, she knelt down and wrapped her arms around the seven-year-old. "I wager you shall be the best of all the lads to come."

"I shall?"

"I am certain of it. You have a good heart, Dughall MacGreagor, and great lads are those with a good heart. Yet, you must not let too many see what is in your heart. You must keep your sorrow a secret and show it only to the ones you hold dearest."

"Like you?"

Catrina hugged him a second time. "Aye, like me. For others, you must appear strong even when you are sad. Can you do it?"

Dughall squared his shoulders. "Aye."

"Then you are wise as well as brave. Now, fetch me some heather, for I need to make a new broom." She smiled when he dashed out the door as fast as his little legs would carry him. Soon, all the children had gone back outside, either to see the new puppies, or to tend the last of their chores.

*

The next day, the women saw to their wash, the men worked in the garden, the children played, the dogs chased the cats, and Catrina finally had time to take a look at the new puppies. The mother Scottie had found a way to keep her young ones safe in a hollowed-out place under the eve of a large rock. The litter consisted of five tiny pups with their eyes still closed. Three were solid black and two were completely white. She stroked the mother dog first, reached for the smallest black one and held the softness of its fur against her face.

With Wallace needed to work on the stonewall, Stefan's younger sons, Niall, Beatan, and Carson, took turns sitting on the wall to watch for Brodies. At only nine, Carson could stand up to watch and still be well hidden behind the branches of the tree, but it was dreary work. Occasionally, Wallace brought a flask of water and let him drink, which helped break the monotony, but only for a time. It was indeed the most tiresome work in the world, but very necessary, and he was proud to be trusted with the responsibility.

Yet when he saw movement on the path that connected the two clans, he couldn't believe his eyes. Carson took a step back and nearly fell off the wall. "Wallace!" he shouted in a shrill voice.

Wallace ran to the wall, grabbed the tree branch, and pulled himself up. He quickly crouched down beside Carson and then asked, "Where?"

Carson pointed to a place a considerable distance away. "There."

It took a moment, but soon Wallace spotted the movement in the trees as well. "Good eyes, Laddie. Keep watching while I tell Father." Wallace jumped down, ran across the courtyard, and headed up the hill to the vegetable garden.

Catrina put the puppy down, stood up, watched, and held her breath. Terror gripped her soul and she could hardly move.

Even before he reached Stefan, Wallace shouted, "Brodies!"

Stefan threw down his shovel and hurried to meet his son halfway. "How many?"

"I cannae tell yet. Shall I ring the gong, Father?"

Stefan turned his son around and started down the hill beside him. "Nay, we best not let them know we have seen them. Go quickly back, watch and send your brothers and sisters to the keep." Stefan let out a shrill whistle, got the attention of the others and pointed toward the Brodie village. An instant later, the MacGreagor women gathered their children and ran for the Keep, while the men rushed to their cottages to better arm themselves. Once more, they went to their designated hiding places.

Yet, Catrina did not move. She watched as her father came back out of the castle fully armed, and still, she remained where she was.

When all was ready, Stefan walked to the wall, and looked up at Wallace. "How many?"

"Two, Father, and the first wears many jewels."

"'Tis Laird Brodie and he comes without his usual guard?"

"I can see no others, Father," Wallace admitted.

"They do not come to fight with only two, then. Watch for more, son, in case they lay a trap for us."

"Aye, Father." When he glanced around, Catrina was still standing near the litter of puppies. "Catrina, see to the children."

She took a forgotten breath. With only two Brodies coming, she didn't see why she had to be inside. She was only a year younger than Wallace, and she could fight as well as any of the women. Even so, she obeyed her father. She might have rushed up to the third floor this time, but the cliff behind the castle blocked any possible view of the Brodie path. Instead, she went to the second floor to get her bow and her sheath of arrows. Just as she started down the stairs, Kenna was coming up.

"I wish to see this time too," said Kenna.

"How brave you have become. Very well, see from the second floor if you can. I am forced to wait with the others below where 'tis doubtful I can see a thing." She had only just come down the stairs when Dughall rushed to her and wrapped his arms around her legs. She harshly removed his arms and knelt down. "Ye must not cling to me, for if I am forced to fight, I need be unbound. Do you hear me?"

Dughall hung his head and pouted. "Aye."

"Sit on the floor with the others and make not a sound." She watched him hurry back and sink to his knees beside his sister. He was still pouting, but she could deal with that later.

The bottom floor of the Keep was the safest place to be, unless there was a fire. Not having windows big enough to climb out of, meant they could be easily trapped. However, the year she was born, Stefan and the men dug an escape tunnel, complete with a trap door in the floor. Two of the women had already lifted the door out of the floor just in case. The women most proficient with a bow and arrow went to their designated slots in the wall and got ready to fight.

Catrina did the same. The height of her slot made it possible to shoot a man on a horse in the chest…if she had the nerve to do it. She placed the blunt end of the arrow against her bowstring, rested the tip on the bottom of her slot, and then glanced back to check on the children. They had practiced it time and again until even the little ones knew just what to do, but they were scared and she didn't blame them. Nevertheless, they were all behaving and so far, everything was going just as planned. Catrina turned back to watch just as the dogs began to bark. It wouldn't be long now.

*

As he had before, Stefan took up his defensive position in front of the castle, but he did not draw his sword, it was not yet time. When he looked to his son for news, Wallace only held up two fingers and it appeared it was not a trap…at least not yet. "Lower your weapons, lads," He commanded, "'tis but two. Let us not be the ones to start a war."

They did as they were told. Every eye watched the end of the stonewall, and at last, the two Brodies rounded the end of it, and slowly walked their horses toward Laird MacGreagor.

Inside, Catrina had no intention of lowering her weapon. Surprisingly, she had an excellent view of what was happening outside, and no longer doubted she had the courage to shoot the man who tried to kill her father. The day may have taken her grandfather, but it would not take her father, not if she had anything to say about it. She narrowed her determined eyes and slightly repositioned her arrow.

Laird Brodie was a round man, having taken too much pleasure from what his vast lands had to offer in the way of food. As well, he wore the wealth gained from selling men into slavery in the form of jewels imbedded in his belt, in his shoes, around his neck, and on nearly every finger. His hair was a dusty brown, and he wore a beard trimmed round on the bottom that unkindly emphasized the roundness of his face. His eyes were brown, and his expression was firmly set as he ignored the barking dogs and drew his horse closer to Stefan.

The man with him was far more interested in the castle, slowly looked up at the second floor and then at the third. He suspected there were at least ten arrows pointed at his chest, and when he spotted the tip of one sticking out of a slot on the first floor, he didn't bother to warn his laird. Instead, his lips curved into a curious smile.

Laird Brodie didn't bother to dismount. "You are the MacGreagor Laird? I had not heard that. As I recall, you are as strong as ten lads." Laird Brodie barely paused long enough to take a breath. "I wish to see this strength again, but not today. Today, I come to hear if Laird Macoran has passed."

There was no point in lying to the one man Stefan hated most in the world – the very man who had enslaved him years ago. News of Laird Macoran's death would spread from hunter to hunter soon enough, so he ignored the question completely. Instead, Stefan narrowed his eyes. "You shall see my strength the day I put you in the ground."

Laird Brodie chuckled. "Still upset, are you? Am I at fault so long as there are lads willing to pay for other lads? I say not. If you must hate, hate not me, but the lad who bought you."

"How easily you shed your guilt."

"I have no guilt to shed. I merely sought to make a profit. Even a Viking can see the benefit of a fine profit, and you enriched my father more than most. 'Tis a pity you lived, MacGreagor, for the day may come when I shall have to fight you."

Stefan's rage was steadily increasing, and there was nothing he would have liked better than to yank the man down and strangle him. Nevertheless, he kept his fury in check. "I shall gladly fight you now."

"Now," Laird Brodie scoffed, "on the day of mourning for Laird Macoran? Come now; have you no regard for the man who married my sister? Poor Agnes was set aside so he could marry your wife's mother. I find it very hard to forgive him for that, but I shall speak no more ill of the dead. As for you, I should derive far more pleasure from killing you in front of my people. They so enjoy a good fight, and while others may fear you, I do not."

"Is your lad not witness enough?" Stefan asked.

"My son, you mean? Branan would like to see you kill me, for he hungers to lead the Brodies. 'Tis a pity he has no wits about him."

Stefan looked at the resentment Laird Brodie's remarks made in the eyes of his son and smiled. "Perhaps he shall kill you for me."

Laird Brodie laughed. "Perhaps he shall." He turned his horse and began to walk it back the way he came. "Perhaps he shall, once he is brave enough, MacGreagor. Perhaps he shall."

As soon as the Brodies were out of sight, William said, "Let me kill him."

"Nay, for his lads will be honor bound to fight us and we cannae win against so many. There are better ways to rid ourselves of evil. First, we bury my father-in-law and make a new alliance with the lad the Macoran's choose as their laird."

"So long as it is not Ronan?"

"Aye, so long as it is not Ronan. If it is, we shall be forced to accept him. Our alliance with the Limond and the Macoran is the only reason Laird Brodie does not attack."

*

Catrina slowly released the tension in her bowstring, slipped her arrow back in the sheath and took a forgotten breath. Her courage had not yet been fully tested, but now she was convinced she could fight if it came to that. She went to the door, unbolted it, and opened it wide. "Father, may we come out now?" She waited for his nod, and then stood aside so all the relieved women and children could go back outside.

Her work was behind, which was a good thing. Preparing the evening meal, she hoped, would take her mind off her sorrow. It didn't work very well, for the grief still laid heavy on her heart. Dughall came inside twice for another hug and the truth be told, she needed it as badly as he did. Long ago, she decided there was some sort of magic healing in the human touch, and never had she needed it more than on this day.

*

When they were not cooking, washing, gathering eggs, and helping in the vegetable garden, Catrina and Kenna sometimes found time to share a few golden moments in the evenings. Soon, the sun would be down. The little ones would need to be put to bed, and there were always chores to do at night, such as mending, making belts, and churning milk into cheese.

Just now, however, they sat on the log at the edge of the courtyard and watched the yellow and orange reflection of the sunset on the shimmering water of the loch. A gentle breeze made ripples, the dogs scared a flock of Graylag geese into taking flight, and seeing the beauty of it all was a soothing end to a completely retched day.

Their attention was soon drawn to two of the three unmarried men, as they carried more stones to the wall in preparation for the next day's work. In their cottages at night, the men made candles, fashioned warm coats out of animal furs, and made shoes and leather belts. Not a scrap of leather went to waste. They made basket straps to hang over the backs of horses, and small pouches for salt, spices, and valuables. Belts that did not fill their own needs were used as barter for tools and weapons. What the unmarried men didn't have much time for was flirting, except for an occasional look and a smile.

When Kenna noticed Grant looking at her, she quickly looked away so he would not know she had been watching him. She brushed a leaf off her long, woolen skirt and frowned. "Can the Brodies not just attack us and get it over with?"

Catrina's mouth dropped. "What a frightful thing to say."

"'Tis not frightful. 'Tis how I feel. All our lives we have fretted over them and still they do not attack."

"Aye, but you may get your wish now that grandfather has passed." At last, Catrina had said something about it aloud, and it sounded foreign somehow. She was his favorite, and each time they went to visit the Macoran village, Laird Macoran took special care to see that she had a good meal and more than her share of his affection. She was going to miss that most of all, for few were the times her father had time just for her.

"Are you going to cry?" Kenna asked watching her friend's sad eyes.

"Nay, the children of Stefan MacGreagor dinna cry."

"My father is the same, but do they not make exceptions when someone we love passes?"

"Father dinna cry when Mother passed."

"Aye, but when he dinna, were you not being brave for his sake?"

"Perhaps. If he had cried, we all would have, but…"

"But a Viking never cries."

"Aye." Catrina looked up the hill. Her father was still hard at work turning the soil in the vegetable garden, even in the diminishing light. "Leastwise, not that Viking, and he's likely the only one we shall ever know."

"Your father is quite handsome…for an elder, that is."

"Is he? I had not thought of that."

"I wonder why he dinna marry again?"

"He loved my mother with his whole heart. Perhaps he finds he cannae love another."

"What will he do though, when you marry?"

Catrina stared at her friend. "I suppose I shall be expected to care for his children as well as my own. There, you see, I am never to have a moment's peace – not until they lay me in the ground."

"I see not what you can do about it. Marriage and children are the way of the world."

Catrina abruptly stood up. "Not my world…not for ten years, at least." With that, she yelled for the little ones to go inside, followed them into the Keep and closed the door.

Still seated on the log, Kenna waited to see if Grant would finally come talk to her, now that she was alone. She waited and waited, but he did not. On the other hand,

Donahue looked at her twice and Garth once. That must mean something, but what? She sighed, got up, and went home. Home was the cottage across the garden and closest to the castle. It was convenient not only for Kenna, but for William, her father, and the second in command. On the other hand, it was so close that when her mother yelled for her, she had few excuses for not responding.

She darted inside, rushed to the window, and peeked out just to see which of the men had been watching her. It appeared none of them had. Disappointed, she puffed her cheeks and went to help her little sister get ready for bed.

# CHAPTER 5

The brothers were nearly out of food, and were low on water when Karr turned the ship due west, instead of sailing southwest as Anundi instructed. If they didn't find land soon, any land at all, they would surely die, and it would all have been for naught. Tired, hungry, and with a thirst they dared not fully quench, they spent the night lying on the floor of the ship certain they were awaiting death. That is, until just after dawn when a seagull landed on the dragon's head.

At first, Karr thought he was seeing things. He slowly raised himself to a sitting position, reached over and tugged on Hani's arm. "Can you see it, lad?"

Hani slowly opened one eye and then the other. "See what?"

"Up there," he said, slowly raising his hand and pointing.

As soon as he saw it too, Hani found he had more strength left than he thought, suddenly got to his feet, and scared the squawking bird away. Soon, all the brothers were wide awake. They crawled into their seats and eagerly awaited word, while Hani slowly scanned the horizon for any hint of land. At length, he sadly shook his head.

"Aye, but we are close," said Karr. "We must be." He headed for the stern, untied the rudder handle, and then gauged the position of the sun. It was already directly behind his back, just where he wanted it to be. "We best wash up if we are to be welcomed ashore."

"We may wear our clean clothes finally?" Obbi asked.

"Aye, we must make Grandfather proud."

"Clean clothes to die in," Steinn mumbled. He had not forgotten the giant black and white fish for one single moment, and bathing meant going *out there* in the water. If they managed to survive that, they still had the Scots to contend with. In fact, he fully expected to die before he even set foot on Scotland.

Steinn offered to keep watch, while one at a time, the brothers stripped down, climbed over the side of the ship, and used soap pilfered in a Viking raid to wash their hair and their bodies. Once they were back in the ship, each happily removed the clothing they kept clean and dry in their leather sacks, put on their linen underclothes, their tunics, belts, long pants, and lastly, their fine leather shoes. The brothers let the wind dry their hair, untangled it with combs made of bones, tied it back, and used their finely sharpened daggers to trim beards in the water's reflection. It was not easy, considering the movement of the ship, but they managed not to cut themselves.

They were as presentable as they were ever going to be – all except Steinn.

"Brother, are you not going to bathe?" Karr asked.

When Steinn looked up, each of his brothers were staring at him. "I care not to go in the water."

"He is bashful," Nikolas teased.

"He is not going ashore after all? Pity that," Obbi added. "Fear not, Steinn, you may stay in the ship and we shall toss food and water to you each day, unless we forget."

"Aye," said Hani, "and we might forget. I, for one, shall be busy taking a wife. 'Tis a great pity, for many a heart shall be broken for want of you." Hani ignored Steinn's glare, and enjoyed the laughter of his brothers instead. His eyes sparkled, although he did not so much as smile.

"I say we throw him in," Almoor suggested.

"Clothes and all?" Obbi asked.

"Touch me not, brothers," Steinn warned.

Karr set his jaw. "I, the commander of this ship, command you bathe, lest you shame us all."

It took a few moments, but at last, Steinn relented and took off his clothes. He took the fastest dip in the ocean of any of the brothers, and hardly got the soap out of his hair before he climbed back in the ship. The brothers knew better than to laugh at him, hid their smiles, and concentrated instead on leaning out to look for land.

Karr too watched for land. Instead of fear or foreboding, he felt inexplicable joy. The long journey had been hard, and being joyful was certainly warranted, but there was something more...something that made his heart want to leap out of his chest. It had to be the nearness of the woman he would love, indeed already loved the way his father loved his mother.

All he had to do was find land – and then find her.

*

Nearly all of the MacGreagors wanted to attend the funeral, but with the threat of a Brodie attack and the garden to prepare for planting, it was better that they stayed home and kept watch. Stefan put William in charge and Kenna offered to watch the children so Catrina could go.

It was time then. Stefan mounted his horse, waited until they were mounted, and then led his two oldest children, Wallace and Catrina, toward the Macoran village to witness the burial of their grandfather. The path from the castle went around the loch to the east, and then split with one part leading to a bridge across the river, and the other part to the Macoran village. They were quiet as they walked their horses past cottages on farms with land that was also being prepared for the spring planting. Most of the Macoran farmers had already gone to the village to pay their respects, but those that had not, paused to reverently bow their heads as the MacGreagors passed. The path ran along the edge of a hill, and on the other side of the farms, was the river that separated the Limond and the Macoran land, both villages of which sat on the shore of the North Sea.

It was a solemn ride indeed, but Catrina had a question. Seldom did she have time alone…or almost alone with Stefan, and now was as good a time as any to ask. "Father, how am I to choose the right husband?"

"You must wait until you love him."

"How will I know if I love him?"

"You shall know. 'Tis a much stronger love than what you feel for others, and even for me," Stefan answered.

"I shall never love anyone more than you, Father."

"Aye, but you shall, and someday soon. The kind of love I speak of is a yearning far greater than hunger or thirst. 'Tis a need so strong, it cannae be denied."

"Is that how you loved my mother?" she asked.

"Aye. Kannak was life to me, just as her children are life to me now. Yet, you cannae consider love alone, for one can love and yet choose a husband or wife unwisely. You must make your mind rule your heart and be certain of his love as well."

"How can I be certain?"

"Well, a lad who loves you will not make idle promises, nor will he threaten you."

"Threaten me?" she gasped.

Stefan considered the best way to explain it. "Suppose he says he will harm someone if you do not choose him. Listen not to him and come to me instead. If he can win you by threats, 'tis just the beginning. You shall be a slave to him, for fear he harms someone you love if you dinna obey him. 'Tis not a life I choose for my daughters."

Wallace listened intently too. "When may I marry, Father?"

"A lad must wait until he is able to care for his family. In a clan, we all work to supply our needs, but a lad must be able to care for a family even without a clan."

"Without a clan?" Wallace huffed. "That shall never happen."

"I pray you are right." When they reached the place where the foot of the hill began to curve, Stefan halted his horse and looked up the path that led to the top. It was on that very hill that he first laid eyes on his wife, and he had not been there since she passed. He would not see it this time either, he decided, and urged his horse onward.

Macoran land was situated in a wide *L* shape, and the closer they got to the village, the narrower the land and the wider the river. On the other side of the *L* shape, the land stretched northward along the eastern coast of Scotland, and it was on that side of the hill that the clan buried their dead. It was also there that Stefan buried his wife, for she was a Macoran before she became a MacGreagor. He had not been there since she passed either, and he was not looking forward to it now.

At last, they rounded the corner and entered the village. In the center was a two-story Keep complete with a large courtyard, stables and storage sheds on the far side. Cottages surrounded the courtyard, and where the mouth of the river emptied into the sea, small fishing boats awaited the men who daily caught salmon to sell to the English. Several yards of cleared land lay between the cottages and the ocean, and at the edge, the Macorans had made a wall of piled rocks to help protect them from marauding Vikings. The two foot barrier normally did little but slow the Vikings down a bit.

The courtyard also served as a market place, although they had not brought out their tables and saleable goods. This day, they had silently gathered in the courtyard to honor their beloved Laird. None had forgotten the many ways he protected the clan and the lengths to which he was willing to do it.

As the three MacGreagor's rode their horses to the center of the courtyard, the Viking's daughter turned the head of every man in the village. Some had not seen her since she became a woman, and found her exceptionally handsome – so much so, more than a few wives were seen elbowing their husbands. Catrina ignored them all, slid down off her horse, and followed her father up the steps, across the wooden walkway and into the Macoran Keep.

ip

She knew the Keep well, for she had come to it often as a child.

Laird Jeffers Limond and his wife were already there, having come to pay their respects to an old friend. Others inside the Keep included Laird Macoran's dearest friends and members of his counsel. Stefan nodded to each and then walked with his son and daughter to the center of the room. Rows of candles sat on the table surrounding Laird Macoran's wooden burial box. Inside the box, the elder man with bright red hair looked peaceful, with his arms proudly folded. The emerald and diamond rings that signified his station in life remained on his fingers. The silver goblet from which he drank lay on one side of him and his polished and glistening sword lay on the other.

Stefan hung his head, closed his eyes and began a silent prayer.

Catrina had already made up her mind not to cry, but when she glanced at her grandfather's lifeless body, she struggled to keep her composure. That is, until she spotted the smirking Ronan Macoran standing against the back wall. In the candle light, his hair looked nearly black and his green eyes reminded her of a hostile cat preparing to pounce. Instead of pointed, his short beard was squared off on the bottom, but it didn't change the shape of his usual goofy grin. Determined to ignore him, she looked away, but she could feel his eyes on her body and found it detestable.

When Stefan finished his silent prayer, he crossed himself in the tradition of his faith and then looked at the wall above the burial box. Amid several other weapons was a sword Stefan knew well from his childhood. It had a golden handle and a wide, flat blade that was sharpened well enough to go through a man's torso with ease. Years ago, it was left behind after the Viking battle that killed his father. It was indeed Anundi's sword. Anundi was his father's best friend, and now the sword rightfully belonged to him.

Stefan smiled as he remembered Laird Macoran's taunting. He refused to give the sword to him until Stefan managed to save ten lasses. In all his years, he still had not managed to save but one, with the help of a mysterious black stallion, and she was his beloved wife. He walked to the wall, carefully took the sword down, removed the sheath, and examined the flat blade. It remained without dint, chip, or blemish.

"'Tis a Macoran sword, MacGreagor," said Ronan from the far side of the room.

Without even turning around, Stefan asked, "Shall we not fight to the death?" He took hold of the sword's handle and slowly turned to face his challenger. His narrowed blue eyes glistened in the candle light and several in the room took a step back.

Ronan Macoran was a stout enough man and ten years Stefan's junior, but before that moment, he had forgotten just how large the Viking was. Yet, for a man with his mind set on becoming the next laird, backing down would not do either. "I have no wish to fight you until after the burying," he said at length, "but perhaps a trade?"

"What sort of trade?" Stefan asked.

"The sword for your daughter."

Stefan slowly grinned. "I would not trade my daughter for a sword."

"What would you trade her for?"

"She shall not be traded, not to the likes of you – not for the sword and the fishing boats, together with all of the Macoran land."

Astonished, Catrina looked from Ronan to her father and back again. Had she not rejected Ronan often enough already? As she recalled, she even kicked him in the shins a time or two, and tried to cut him with her sword at least twice. Was he still senseless enough to ask for her? The thought of being his wife was far too appalling even to contemplate.

Ronan walked closer to the candle light, and as he did, the red in his hair began to show. He boldly sneered at Stefan. "No lass is worth all that, MacGreagor."

Stefan put the sword back in its sheath, pushed his own sword back, and tied the strings of Anundi's sword around his waist. "'Tis why you shall never be a happy lad, Ronan. You place no value on a wife or a clan."

"I value them well enough. What will you do when I set about to make an alliance with the Brodies?"

Stefan was expecting that. "To make an alliance, you would likely have to marry one of Laird Brodie's daughters. I hear neither is greatly sought after."

"Perhaps, but think of your own peril. For a lad who claims to cherish his people, you do not choose well at all. Should I align my clan with the Brodies, your clan would surely perish. Give me your daughter and we shall continue to live in peace."

Stefan glanced at Laird Limond, saw the slight grin on his face and suspected he was quite enjoying himself. "You imagine yourself laird of the Macorans, but you do not yet have the clan's pledge to follow you. Therefore, your demands and your threats are quite without notice. Both the sword and my daughter go with me. For both, I am content to wait until you have gathered the courage to fight me."

Ronan's face was beginning to turn red with anger. "Dare you…" The door abruptly opened and he turned to see who it was.

"The priest has arrived," a man uttered, standing aside so the priest could enter.

"We best get on with it, then," Ronan said. He turned and walked out the door.

"Blatherskite," Stefan muttered loud enough for everyone to hear. It was perhaps not appropriate, but when he called Ronan a silly talker, it brought a smile to more than one face. He and his children stood back while the Macorans moved the candles away, put the lid on the box, and nailed it shut with iron pegs. Next, the six chosen men lifted it up and rested the box on their shoulders.

The priest led the way, followed by Stefan and his children, Laird Limond and his wife, and then the other closest relatives, of which there were many. All that remained of the clan fell in behind. Normally, the next laird would walk directly behind the box, but apparently, Ronan decided not to push his luck, and brought up the rear instead.

A bright sun shone above as they slowly and reverently crossed the courtyard and turned north up the beach toward the cemetery. Walking three and four across, the line stretched all the way from the center of the village, up the coast to the graveyard. The Priest patiently waited until all who wanted to be close enough to hear, had arrived.

The service was no different than that of the common man; although the headstone would be considerably larger, once it was carved. The men carrying the box, carefully set it across ropes held by other men, and together, they reverently lowered the box into the hole. Once the ropes were pulled out, they went to take their place among the clan.

And still Catrina did not shed a tear. Perhaps she would when they got home, and could have a few precious moments alone. Just now, however, she could still feel Ronan's eyes on her. She didn't bother to learn where he was, for that would only encourage him. Always before, he had been just a source of annoyance. Today, she feared, all that had changed. Hopefully, the Macorans were wise enough not to make him their laird. Surely, they would not.

The priest was nearly finished when the near silence was broken by the sound of the Macoran gong. The people virtually froze to count the gongs and when it continued, beat after beat, there was no doubt in anyone's mind what it meant. They turned in unison to look out across the sea.

"Vikings," someone whispered, and soon every eye widened, even those of the priest.

*

"Run!" came a collective uproar. Parents grabbed their children and began to race back to the village. Some of the men were well armed, but others were not and were caught completely off guard. They ran for their weapons, grabbed their shields, and then took up positions facing the water behind the wall of rocks.

Soon, only Stefan, his children, Laird Limond and his wife, remained where they were. Little more than the top of the sail was visible at first, but there was no doubt the ship was headed straight for them.

"My eyes do not see well these days, MacGreagor," said Laird Jeffers Limond. "How many ships are there?"

"But one so far," Stefan answered.

"Shall you know them, Father?" Wallace asked.

"'Tis doubtful, I have not seen the land of the Norsemen in years."

A stout man, nearly the same age as Stefan, Laird Limond had slightly graying brown hair, and it was easy to see he was quite fond of his redheaded wife. He took her hand to reassure her, and then slowly shook his head. "Well, they never seem to tire of attempting to land on our shores. Normally, we can shoot our fire arrows at their ships well enough to persuade them to take their thievery elsewhere. Perhaps we can this time as well. How many now?"

"But one and it has slowed. Perhaps it waits for the others," Stefan answered.

"Shall you fight them, Father," Catrina asked. "Do Viking's fight Vikings?"

"When life is threatened, a Viking fights whomever he must. Come." Stefan saw no need to hurry with the longship still a considerable distance away, but he kept watch as they walked back to the village. He expected more ships to appear on the horizon, and wrinkled his brow when they did not. He stopped, shielded his eyes from the sun with his hand, and carefully examined as much as he could see of the ocean to the north, and then to the south. There were no other ships – at least not yet.

*

Karr couldn't believe it. Before them, lay two villages parted by a river, just as Anundi said, but how was that possible? Surely, they had been off course and likely more than once. With slightly parched lips and for the second time, he lifted his eyes to the heavens. "Thank you, Grandfather."

Hani got to his feet, held on to the bow, leaned out and looked. "The land is green. If they let us, we shall be happy here."

"Aye, if they let us," Steinn muttered. He was more than willing to stay seated and let the others look.

Obbi stayed in his seat too, but hung on and leaned over the side so he could see too. "'Tis not safe. The people already gather on the shore and they are too many."

"Have you a better idea?" Karr asked.

Obbi nodded. "We could put to shore farther north."

"Aye, but how would we find water? Another day or two and we shall surely die. We must have fresh water, brother, and they have a river."

Obbi looked back at the land and licked his lips. "True and I shall happily drink it all."

"Gather your belongings, lads. When we are near enough, we shall take down the sail," Karr commanded.

\*

As they walked toward the village, Laird Limond oddly started to laugh. He couldn't help himself, for Ronan had dashed into the Keep, put on a Viking helmet with a metal nose guard, and come back out. He was the only one wearing a helmet and he looked ridiculous with his shield held out in front of him, his sword already drawn, and most of his face hidden behind the heavy helmet. Twice, Ronan had to shove the helmet up so it wouldn't cover his eyes.

"Would that half my lads were as brave as he," Laird Limond joked to his smiling wife.

Stefan rolled his eyes. "If one ship frightens him, I should like to see what he does when a hundred come." Once they reached the village, the anxious crowd quieted to hear what the two lairds had to say. Stefan turned to his son and daughter. "Stay behind the rocks. If they are bold enough to land, I shall speak to them."

Laird Limond asked, "How many ships now?"

"Just one. They have taken down their sail and I count but seven lads."

"I count seven too, Father," said Wallace.

"Let them come then," said Laird Limond. He looked across the river to see if his men were ready. The pounding of the shield brought the Limonds to the waterfront on their side of the river as well. Each time the Viking's attacked, both clans waited to see where they would try to land. If the attempt was made in front of the Macoran village, the Limonds boarded their barges, crossed the river and fought beside their neighbors. If the opposite was true, the Macorans crossed the river instead. His men looked well prepared and Laird Limond was pleased.

The Macorans watched as the Vikings put their oars in the water and began to steadily row toward them. They rowed in perfect synchronization, but their labors produced little speed.

"They be half dead, I wager," Laird Limond said. As soon as Stefan stepped across the pile of stones, Laird Limond did the same.

"Not as dead as they will be if they come ashore," Ronan loudly boasted.

Stefan ignored him and kept his eyes on the approaching vessel. "They sail a ship built for sixty, and only seven have survived."

Laird Limond looked to the crowd. "Bring water." Four of the men untied their flasks and began to walk toward him.

"Dead lads dinna need water," Ronan shouted.

Laird Limond folded his arms in a huff and turned to stare at the man behind the helmet. The helmet made Ronan's eyes look too close together and it was all Limond could do to keep from laughing out loud. "'Tis for me," he shouted.

"Oh," was all Ronan said. He dropped his sword on the ground, waved his hand in the air, and pointed at Laird Limond. "Water!" he commanded, ignoring the fact that it was already being delivered. Just as quickly, he picked his sword back up, shoved his helmet up, and positioned himself to fight. Fortunately, he could only see straight ahead and didn't notice members of his clan covering their mouths to muffle their laughter.

Laird Limond turned back to watch the longship. "More might be lying on the deck to trick us into thinking there are only seven."

"Aye," Stefan agreed, "but at that speed, they cannae beach the ship well enough. 'Tis too heavy and if they cannae beach it, they must make it through the water before they fight. 'Tis troublesome for lads already weary from the journey."

"Make ready to shoot your fire arrows, lads," Ronan shouted behind them. Just then, he realized he'd forgotten to command them to build the fire in the first place. He dropped his sword again, pulled the helmet off his head and looked around. Sure enough, there was no fire and no one had brought out the store of wool wrapped arrows to set ablaze. Completely exasperated, he put his helmet back on and reached for his sword. "They built no fire," he sighed. "Must I tell them everything to do?" He looked and the ship was still a ways out, but he wasn't taking any chances. "Make ready to fight!"

Exasperated, Stefan closed his eyes and bowed his head for a moment. He turned completely around to look the pretend laird full in the eye. "Shall we not let them attack first? Perhaps they come in peace."

"When have the Vikings ever come in peace?" Ronan scoffed.

"My father would have, had the Macorans not shot their arrows first. We Vikings had no choice but to fight."

"So *you* claim," Ronan shot back.

Stefan glared at the much smaller man. "You shall not fight them this day unless I command it. If you do, I shall kill you myself."

"I do not fear you, MacGreagor." Ronan said it, but the slump of his shoulders said otherwise.

Stefan glanced back at the approaching ship, and then directed his remarks to all the warriors. "'Tis only seven. Since when do the Macoran's kill for the sake of killing? No lad shall die this day save by my command. Agreed?"

"Agreed," the warriors shouted. They put their swords away, laid down their shields, and clasped their hands behind their backs...all but Ronan.

Again, Stefan ignored him, turned back to face the water, and slowly drew Anundi's sword. He turned it upside down, and then held the wide blade in front of his face.

*

Sitting in the stern with his hand on the rudder handle, Karr squinted in the bright afternoon sunlight. It wouldn't be long now until they landed and he knew they would be fortunate indeed if they got the tip of the bow on dry land. It was the best they could do and it would have to be enough. As they neared, he concentrated on the two men standing together in front of the others. One, the one with light hair was considerably taller, and the sword he held before his face glistened in the sunlight. It was a Viking sign of peace, yet he doubted many Scots knew it. It could be a trick, but it didn't matter. The Scots held the lives of the brothers in their hands and they were landing – come what may.

Seated with their backs to the land, his anxious brothers watched the worried expression on Karr's face. As soon as he realized it, he stopped beating cadence with the tip of his sword, brought it to his face, and held it the same way as the stranger on shore. Then he went back to tapping the cadence. They were too tired to go faster and he was tired too, so he didn't demand it of them.

"Could be a trap," Hani said.

"Aye, but the sword he holds has a golden grasp."

"Anundi's sword?" Steinn asked. He was so surprised that he almost stopped rowing and had to hurry to get back in sync.

"Could be." Karr was uncertain too. He carefully watched, hoping that if he detected a trap, he could turn the ship in time to avoid a landing. He watched, but he saw nothing suspicious, and soon it was too late to turn the ship. They were headed straight for the man with the sword, and when he could see the other warriors well enough, he noticed only one had his sword drawn.

Closer and closer they came, and when he thought it was time, he yelled. "Lift your oars, lads, and hang on." A few moments later, the bow of the ship hit dry land with a thud and abruptly stopped, harshly jerking the brothers first backward and then forward.

# CHAPTER 6

The people were so still, even those hiding at the foot of the hill could hear the flat bottom hull screech across the sand.

Then there was complete silence.

Waves lapped against the side of the ship, a seagull squawked as it flew overhead, but none of the Vikings made a move. Curious women and children peeked around Macoran men, and others began to ease closer to get a better look.

Exhausted and convinced they were not going to die right away, Karr finally let loose of the rudder handle and bowed his head. When he finally raised it again, he saw only one face – the face of an angel with long blonde hair and eyes the color of a pristine Norwegian lake. The leap in his heart told him he had found her, but was it possible, or had the lack of food and water made him go completely daft? When she lowered her eyes, Karr forced himself to look away.

The tall one with the sword, seemed to be the Scot's leader, so when Karr spoke, he spoke to Stefan. "We come in peace."

Stefan slowly lowered the sword. "You speak Gaelic?"

"Aye, an old Scottish lass taught us."

Karr stood up and slowly made his way to the bow of the ship. He lifted one leg over the side and then the other, until he sat on the rim. When he jumped down, landing on the hard earth after so many days at sea made his knees buckle and he nearly fell. As soon as he regained his balance, he said, "I am Karr Olney and they are my brothers."

"There be but seven of you?" Stefan asked.

"Aye. May they come ashore?"

Stefan nodded. "We shall not harm them."

Relieved, Karr nodded to his brothers, and then helped steady each of them when they jumped down. The crowd remained quiet and watched as the unusually large men lined up facing Laird MacGreagor and Laird Limond. Each seemed just as curious about the Scots, as the Scots were about them.

Catrina was fascinated as well. Many times her father talked about the hardships of crossing the sea, and she expected them to look far more unkempt than they did. She didn't doubt they were weaker than before they sailed, but they did not seem too worse for wear.

"I am Stefan, Laird of the MacGreagors and son of Donar, commander of the Viking ship *Sja Vinna*."

Each of the brothers smiled, except Hani, who never smiled. "We have found you," said Karr. He was even taller than Stefan at nearly six feet, ten inches, and he pointed at his brothers, one at a time. "He is Hani, the second eldest, and Steinn is the third. Magnus is forth, Nikolas fifth, Almoor, sixth, and the wee one is Obbi."

Obbi leaned forward, narrowed his eyes and glared at his brother. It made Catrina smile and some in the crowd laugh, for he was hardly small. Pleased with the attention, Obbi smiled back at the people. He'd never seen so many with red hair in his life. When he spotted the strange one in the Viking helmet, he curiously tipped his head to the side, but he said nothing.

"Might that be Anundi's sword?" Karr asked.

"Aye," Stefan answered.

"We have traveled far to see it again. We are Anundi's grandsons and he sent us to seek sanctuary with you."

"Where is Anundi?" Stefan asked, finally putting the sword back in its sheath.

Karr bowed his head. "He has passed."

"I am sorely grieved to hear it."

Laird Limond cleared his throat. "I am laird Limond of the clan across the river. These are Macorans and they have just buried their laird. You look a bit thirsty, lads." He leaned down, picked up two of the water flasks and handed one to Hani and the other to Karr. It was then that they did an odd thing. The older brothers passed the flasks down so the younger could drink first. It was touching and impressed several in the Macoran clan, especially the unmarried women.

While the younger brothers drank, Stefan switched to speaking the language of the Norsemen, so no one would know what he was asking. "Are you sought after?"

Karr nodded. "Perhaps, but we saw no other ships."

Stefan switched back to Gaelic. "Have you eaten?"

"If you can call it that," Hani answered. "'Twas two days hence."

"Bring food," Laird Limond shouted.

"Nay," Ronan yelled, "let the Vikings eat dirt if they are hungry."

Hani wrinkled his brow and looked around. "From where does the voice come?"

"From inside my father's Viking helmet," Stefan answered, nodding in Ronan's direction. "He fancies himself the next Macoran laird. We pay him no mind."

Hani searched the crowd until his eyes landed on the man who appeared to be hiding behind two others. "I can see why. His head be too small for the helmet."

Talking about him as though he was not there raised Ronan's ire. He tried to think of another command, but could not come up with one. Instead, he simply glared at Stefan, who he noticed, had his back disrespectfully to him.

As soon as he finished drinking, Karr handed the flask back to Laird Limond. "We best burn the ship."

Laird Limond had another idea. "I say we hide it upriver instead."

"Tis a heavy ship," Karr pointed out, "'twill take many horses and lads to pull it up river."

"We have many horses and lads," Laird Limond pointed out, "'Tis a shame to burn it when we can discover how 'tis built instead."

"I'll not see a Viking ship on *my* river," Ronan bellowed.

Laird Limond had heard just about enough from him, and once more slowly turned around. "'Tis not *your* river, not by any count."

Karr paid no attention to the argument. Instead, he was worried. "Can your lads hide it quickly?"

"Quickly?" Limond asked. "Oh, I see, the others are not far behind."

Karr looked at Stefan and then back at Laird Limond. "We know not where they are, but if the ship is seen, others will surely come."

"True." Laird Limond agreed, and then took a moment to ponder the idea. "Very well, 'tis a pity, but we best burn it." He stepped back across the pile of rocks. "Lads, build a fire and prepare to sink the ship." He was pleased when several of the men obeyed.

"Nay," Ronan shouted, "let them go back to the sea and drown."

Karr stared at the much smaller man who was trying his best to look ferocious. "Who be the laddie?"

Stefan grinned, "'Tis Ronan and he has laid claim to Anundi's sword."

"Has he now?" Karr looked at Ronan again and raised an eyebrow. "I will fight him for you. I've not drawn blood in almost three months."

"Perhaps when you are rested," said Stefan, "we shall spar for the right to fight him. I'd not give up the pleasure easily."

"If you wish," Karr said. "May we find sanctuary with you?"

"Perhaps," Stefan answered.

Karr wrinkled his brow. "Perhaps?"

"To join Clan MacGreagor, you must live by my edict."

"What edict is that?" Karr asked.

"First, a lad who forces a lass shall be put to death."

Karr shrugged, "We seek willing wives. We agree, MacGreagor."

"'Tis more," said Stefan. "A lad who harms a lass or a child out of anger shall also put to death."

"I see. Is there a third edict?"

"Aye, one more. A lass shall choose her husband, and he who asks for her must abide by her decision."

Hani's mouth dropped. "What's this? You allow the lass to choose?"

Stefan raised an eyebrow. "Catrina come here." He waited while she stepped over the rocks and came to stand beside him. "This be my daughter and I wish her to be happy. I say no lad shall have her against her will. What say you?"

For a second time, Karr looked into the eyes of the blonde beauty, holding her gaze for several long seconds before he answered. "I would kill the lad who forced her to marry against her will."

"Then we are agreed?" Stefan asked.

"We are agreed," said Karr. He didn't notice the incredulous look on the faces of his brothers. All he could see was Catrina as she turned and went back across the rocks.

"I do *not* agree!" shouted Ronan. "Catrina shall marry me, like it or not. Furthermore, no Viking shall marry a Macoran. We kill Vikings; we do not give them our daughters."

Karr took a deep breath and slowly let it out. "Dinna make me fight you, laddie."

Ronan raised his sword and valiantly pointed it at the Viking. "Dare you call me laddie?"

One look at the scowl on Karr's face and the people nearest Ronan began to scatter. He did not hesitate, nor did he draw his sword. Instead, Karr stepped over the rocks and with long strides straight for Ronan. He stopped only inches away and with the back of his hand, shoved Ronan's sword aside. "Dare you challenge me, laddie?"

Terrified, Ronan jerked his head to the side to see how many of his men were there to protect him. When he did, the helmet slipped down over his eyes. "Kill him!" he commanded, but it was too late. He felt the giant's hands under his armpits just before he began to fly through the air. Abruptly, his back hit the trunk of a tree. The sword flew out of his hand, the helmet rang like a bell, and soon his world went black – which was a good thing, for he did not hear all the laughter.

Karr slowly turned to see if he had any other challengers. There were none, so he walked back across the rocks. "Gather your things, Lads," he said to his brothers. "We be MacGreagors now."

Behind him, two Macoran warriors went to see if Ronan was dead. While one removed the helmet, the other put his ear to Ronan's chest. "He lives," the second man said. They left him in a sitting position against the tree and went to watch the Vikings again. Three of the brothers were already inside the ship, tossing their sacks out to the others. There was one sack, however, they moved with greater care and gently handed down to Karr.

"We could use the sail," Stefan mentioned.

"And the water barrels?" Obbi asked. When Stefan nodded, he dumped what little water remained into the ocean and tossed the barrels out.

Catrina watched them cut the ropes to the sail and fold up the large sheet of material. It too, they tossed on the shore and when the Macorans brought baskets of straw, the brothers emptied the baskets in the center of the ship and then tossed them on the sand. Obbi, the wee one his brother said, thought to climb the mast, pull down the wind bird, and hand it out as well. At last, everything was on land and all that remained was to push the ship out to sea, shoot the arrows and watch it burn. With several Macoran's helping, the ship was easily pushed away, the arrows were shot and soon, black smoke began to rise into the air.

With nothing left to do, the brothers found a place to sit on the rocks and watched their ship burn. Karr thanked the Macoran woman who gave them hot bread cakes to eat, and savored every bite of the fresh food that he was not convinced they would ever eat again. Another woman brought them a flask of wine. Scottish wine was a bit sweeter than the wine in Norway, but he wasn't going to complain about that either. The Scots had accepted them and that's all that mattered. Twice, he looked to see where Catrina was, but several men had gathered between them and he couldn't see her.

For a time, he was concerned that the rising smoke would bring the Vikings. He hadn't said anything to his brothers, but he was certain the Norsemen wouldn't just forgive them and let it go. They left two ships behind, and it would probably take less than a day to load supplies and gather the men needed to give chase. Naturally, they could only guess where the brothers put to shore...unless they could see the smoke. He faithfully watched the horizon, until at last, the fire burned through the hull in the middle of the ship. It began to take on water, and little by little, the drifting ship filled until the fire was out and the ship sank. Even then, Karr kept his eyes on the horizon.

At length, Karr stood up. "Which way?" he asked Stefan.

Seated next to him, Laird Limond stood up too. "Time to take my bonnie lass home, I see. Come for a visit, Stefan, when you can. I suspect we shall have trouble with the Brodies shortly."

"Particularly if Ronan is the next Macoran Laird," Stefan jeered.

"Is he yet alive?" Laird Limond joked.

*

Stefan offered to borrow horses, but the Vikings wanted to walk the stiffness out of their joints. They didn't have that far to go, and if they got tired he reasoned, he could always borrow horses from the farmers along the way. However, to carry the water barrels and the sail, they did need to borrow one horse. The Macorans were certain the unconscious Ronan wouldn't mind if they borrowed his, as long as Wallace brought the mare back. Everyone had a good laugh over that.

Peace with the Vikings was a long way off, but the Macorans agreed these were not such bad sorts after all. More than one unmarried Macoran woman hated to see them go, and not long after the brothers were out of sight, several gathered at the edge of the courtyard to do their most pressing gossiping.

With Stefan and the packhorse in the lead, Catrina rode beside her brother this time, and it wasn't long before she quietly giggled. "I cannae wait to see the look on Kenna's face."

Wallace smiled too. "I cannae wait to see the look on all their faces."

Catrina turned just enough to see behind her. It did not appear any of them resented having to walk. Most of them seemed content to get a good look at the farmland, and occasionally one of them stopped to examine the flowers and leaves of a tall bush he did not find familiar. They had large leather bags slung over their shoulders, and carried three prong spears, bows, arrow sheaths, and their shields. She doubted she could carry half that, but none of them seemed to mind. In fact, they were all smiling, save the one called Hani, who had yet to smile. While the others carried two or three sacks each, Karr had only two, one of which clanked when he walked. It made her curious, but she dare not look at it for long and turned back around. They were handsome men, one and all, she decided, and perhaps she would not have to settle for Grant after all.

*

When they reached the place where the path split near the loch, Stefan, Wallace, and Catrina turned their horses toward the castle just as they always did. They assumed the brothers would follow and none of them thought to look behind them. As soon as she arrived, Catrina slid off her horse and rushed to greet all her brothers and sisters. She gave each a quick hug and then spotted the gawking Kenna. Catrina giggled and went to stand beside her.

Instead of following, the brothers had gone to the edge of the loch and were staring at the glorious abundance of fresh water. Steinn, the brother who balked at washing in the ocean, began it and before long, all the brothers were dropping their sacks and weapons on the bank of the loch. All seven walked into the water together and when they were out far enough, they completely submerged.

Kenna waited and waited, and when they did not immediately resurface, she gasped, "They have drowned themselves!" A moment later, they reappeared and by then, they were nearly halfway across the loch. She breathed a sigh of relief and turned to her best friend. "Are they *all* for me?"

Catrina laughed, "Of course they are. 'Tis a gift from me to you."

"How shall I ever thank you?"

"I'll think of something," Catrina answered.

Kenna's eyes were bright and her heart was all aflutter. "Which do you choose?" she whispered.

Catrina giggled. "I choose not to marry, remember?"

"Aye, but I wager that is about to change. How can it not, with such as these to choose from?"

"You forget; they must choose us first."

Kenna kept her eyes on the brothers, took hold of a lock of her hair and began to twirl it. "What are they called?"

"I dinna remember just now." She couldn't help but watch them too. Perhaps there was one she preferred, but once they swam underwater again and came up, their matching drenched hair made it impossible to tell which was which.

"Well, whatever their names, they are now all wet."

"Aye, and clean. Father says 'tis a long voyage from the land of the Vikings to here, and the salt in the ocean is none too pleasant for bathing."

"They came in a ship?"

"Aye. I have much to tell you. You shall laugh when I tell you about Ronan. First, he…"

*

Stefan's second in command was amazed, just as all the others were. By the time William noticed him, Stefan had handed the reins to the packhorse to Wallace, dismounted and was standing nearby. "Who are they?" William asked.

"They have agreed to be MacGreagors and they are our protection against the Brodies," Stefan answered.

"Ah, I see your point. Can they hunt, for we are in need of good hunters?"

"We are in need of building more cottages now that they are here as well," Stefan added.

"Aye. We are builders, and if they are good hunters, we shall make a fair trade."

"Agreed."

"Should we hide our lasses?" William asked. He had yet to take his eyes off the swimming brothers, for the loch was long and none of them seemed to need rest.

Stefan smiled. "Nay, they have agreed to the edicts."

"Good, for I doubt I could keep Kenna away from them for long."

"'Tis time she married."

"Aye, 'tis time – if by some miracle she can choose wisely."

The Vikings, Stefan noticed, were good swimmers and drank as they swam. He couldn't blame them. He remembered well his first night in Scotland, and how he could not get enough of the fresh, clean water in the river. Yet, how they had the strength to swim amazed even him. All he wanted to do his first night was to sleep in a place that was not constantly rocking.

*

When they reached the other side of the water, the brothers walked out, stood on the shore, and looked back at all the MacGreagors watching them. "Ye should not have agreed to the edicts," said Hani.

"Nay," he should not have," Steinn agreed, shoving wet hair off his face with both hands.

"Have we some place other to go?" Karr asked. When none of them answered, he nodded. "'Tis good land."

"Aye," Obbi agreed, "but we need wives."

"You are too young to marry," Almoor reminded him. "Besides, why would a lass choose us?"

"I can see why none would choose you," Nikolas teased.

"Or you," Obbi shot back, shoving Nikolas back into the water.

Karr didn't interfere. The three youngest enjoyed their bantering and after weeks behaving in a ship, it was good to see them back at it. Instead, he looked across the water at the beauty he hadn't been able to take his mind off of since he first saw her. She captured his attention like no other woman ever had, and just now, she was standing with another woman and a group of children watching them.

Before long, the two youngest brothers finished their jousting and came back on shore.

"Obbi is right," Hani said, his serious expression well intact. "We know nothing of tempting a lass to marry us."

"We shall learn," said Karr. "We shall watch what the MacGreagors do and do likewise."

"I favor Catrina," said Almoor.

"As do I," Nikolas added.

"And me," said Magnus.

"If I am too young," Obbi protested to Karr, "So are Nikolas and Almoor."

"I am older than you," Almoor shot back. He was about to shove his brother when Karr held up his hand to silence them.

"The lass is to choose," Karr reminded them. "Let us not rush. Let us make them glad they have accepted us. We shall work hard, learn their ways, and as we learn, we shall try to tempt a lass to choose us."

Almoor grinned. "I choose Catrina even if I am not old enough. She shall wait for me, I am certain of it."

Karr frowned. "Have you no ears to hear? 'Tis Catrina who shall do the choosing."

Almoor turned to look back across the water. "Not if I tempt her first." He abruptly turned, waded into the water, and began to swim back.

The race was on.

Karr shook his head and puffed his cheeks. There were some things he just couldn't control. Slowly, he waded into the water after his six brothers. He was the biggest, but it didn't mean he moved more easily through the water. For a time, Almoor was in the lead, then Steinn who was soon passed by Magnus. Magnus was about to win, when Obbi grabbed Steinn's leg, and yanked him back. That began it, and the more they tried to outdo one another, the more the MacGreagors laughed and cheered. Even Karr got dunked a time or two when he caught up, and soon six of the brothers were playfully fighting for first place. It was not until they gave up the battle, that they realized Nikolas was standing on the shore not far from Catrina waiting for them. Never had they seen such a satisfied grin on his face.

Nikolas was perhaps not the most handsome of the seven, and he usually didn't win, but this day he did. He bowed first to his brothers and then turned to take another in front of the laughing MacGreagors.

Surrounded by their siblings, Catrina and Kenna laughed too. If this was any indication, life in the MacGreagor village was about to change for the better.

\*

In the trees on the Macoran side of the MacGreagor loch, Muriel Macoran watched the brothers too. Although she did not attend Laird Macoran's burial, she couldn't miss seeing the Vikings walk past her father's farm and hurried to follow. When they laughingly tried to drown each other, she shoved her unruly red hair away from her face, covered her mouth, and giggled.

She would have gone to join in the fun, but for as long as she could remember, she and Kenna had been bitter enemies. Kenna was always accusing her of trying to trick a man, any man, into marriage, and even shooed her away from the MacGreagor village with a broom a time or two. It made no sense to Muriel, for there were plenty of Macoran men to marry if she wanted one that badly. Yet, watching the Vikings made her swoon. No handsomer men had she ever seen, and she might just have to prove Kenna right. Too soon, it was time to tend the cows, so she turned and headed home…but not without pausing a time or two to look back.

\*

"That one?" Catrina asked. "The one with the flat nose?" She sat on the log beside Kenna and watched as Stefan introduced the dripping wet Vikings to the other men and their wives. Of the children, Dughall missed her most, and he would have sat in her lap if she let him, but he was getting too heavy and had to settle for sitting right beside her.

Kenna wrinkled her brow and looked from brother to brother trying to figure out what Catrina was talking about. "They dinna have flat noses."

"They will have, if they dinna stop staring at us."

Kenna laughed. "I fancy them looking, and so do you. We've not got this much attention in our whole lives."

"Aye, but Grant is not pleased. He watches you watching the brothers and shakes his head."

"Grant can marry a Macoran or a Limond and be happy."

"And if he has his heart set on you?"

Kenna lifted her chin. "He should have said so. Now, 'tis too late."

It was Catrina's turn to giggle. "With you, 'tis never too late. You change your mind as often as the wind changes directions."

Kenna folded her arms and took a defeated breath. "'Tis true. Oh, how shall we ever choose?"

"I say you must not rush. Wait until after the next full moon to decide."

"Me? What will you be doing while I am waiting?"

"I shall be caring for all of my father's children, just as I always do."

"If that be the case, I shall have my pick and you can have what is left." Kenna sighed for the tenth or eleventh time in the last hour. "I think I like the tallest one best. What is his name?"

"Darr...or perhaps, Barr. Him you may have and may you be exceedingly happy."

"Well, if you dinna want him, neither do I?"

Catrina teased, "You are so easily persuaded. I shall enjoy watching to see which you marry. I shall enjoy it very much." She got up, took Dughall's hand and headed to the Keep to begin the evening meal. "I missed you today," she told her little brother on the way.

"You did?" a delighted Dughall asked.

"Sorely." She paused at the door to give him a chore. "Would you kindly go to the root cellar and fetch some onions?" Giving him something to do always pleased him, and he happily skipped away. One last time, Catrina glanced at the brothers. Three of the seven were looking at her too, which made her self-conscious, so she hurried inside. "Have they never seen a lass before?" she muttered.

# CHAPTER 7

That evening, after they put their belongings in two of the empty cottages and ate a good meal, the brothers and several of the other men gathered around a campfire in the courtyard to talk. "I long for news from home," Stefan began. He sat on the log between William and Wallace, facing the seven Vikings.

Inside and only after she had all the children in bed, Catrina moved a chair close to one of the slots on the bottom floor of the castle and listened. She hoped to get a good look at each of them, but Karr was the only one in her field of view. She remembered well the way he looked at her while he was still on the ship, and like it or not, she found his attention pleasing. It didn't mean anything, she convinced herself, but she rather liked it. She liked it a lot. Just now, he was talking, so she moved her ear closer to the slot. His deep voice had a calmness to it she also found pleasing.

"The land is worse than when you left," Karr answered. "The people move farther into the mountains and as I said, the hunting yields little. They brave the harsh winters. What else can they do?"

"What of my aunt and her children?" Stefan asked.

"Her children are well, those who have not moved south. It was she who taught us your language. Sadly, she has also passed."

Stefan hung his head in sorrow. "She raised me and I remember her warmly. She was a good lass and I am grieved I dinna see her again."

"She was likely glad to be rid of you," Karr teased. "One less mouth to feed."

Stefan chuckled. "True. I was not yet fifteen when father let me sail with him."

"Anundi told us about the battle and of seeing you again after, but he dinna know what became of you once they sailed away. We are thankful to find you yet alive."

"As am I, I doubted I would be a time or two." Stefan told how the Macorans gave Donar and his men a proper burial at sea. "Laird Macoran was a noble lad, who we put in the ground just before you came. The Macorans are a good and just clan."

"Then we shall honor the Macorans too," said Karr. When he glanced at his brothers, all of them nodded their agreement.

"Save the stupid one," Almoor put in. "Him we shall *not* honor."

"Ronan? I agree," said Stefan, "but 'tis up to the Macorans to choose a laird. He will fight the one they choose and I should like being there to see it, but I am needed here. You are needed here as well. We've a problem with the Brodies."

"Brodies?" Karr asked.

Stefan told them about being enslaved and that it was the Brodies who captured and then sold him.

Karr was indignant. "We shall attack the Brodies in the morning."

"Nay, even with you, they outnumber us fifty to one," said Stefan.

"They be that many?" Magnus asked.

"Aye. We must outwit them if we are to live in peace and I've a plan."

"We are listening," Karr said.

Stefan pointed at the wall and then up the eastern side of the loch. "Near the shore, we have dug out the stones until it is deep enough to swallow a horse. We mean to build the wall to the shore and force the Brodies into the water. The horses shall have to swim, which will give us more time to prepare."

"How often do they attack?"

"They have not...not yet, but they shall if Ronan becomes Laird of the Macoran, and makes an alliance with them by marrying one of Laird Brodie's daughters." Stefan explained the secret passageway out of the Keep, and continued to tell them everything else they needed to know.

*

Catrina moved away from the slot. She had heard her father's plan before and doubted it would work, but it was not her place to say yea or nay. She was more than happy to leave that part of life in the hands of the men. Instead, she climbed the stairs, undressed, and got into bed. She pulled the covers up and thought about the events of the day. How sad she was to say a final goodbye to her grandfather and yet, she had little time to grieve before the brothers came. Was he among them – the man whose arms she could almost feel around her? She could not be sure. She remembered her father's warnings and said them aloud, "Hear no promises, listen to no threats… and let him not be stupid."

Catrina added the last one herself.

Ronan could be a problem she must take seriously. Should he become laird and marry a Brodie, there would be war, and the only way to prevent that from happening was for her to accept him. But oh, how she hated the very thought of it. Perhaps they could flee to another land. Of course, the clans were always fighting over good land and it would not be easy, or so she had heard. Besides, the Macoran would never be foolish enough to keep Ronan as their laird. "Impossible," she muttered. Before long, her eyes began to droop and she fell asleep.

*

The next morning, Catrina awoke to the wondrous smell of hot porridge. Not one of her brothers and sisters were in her bed, not even seven-year-old Dughall, who was always hungry, and almost always there when she awoke. It was not good to have favorites, but Dughall was an exception. He needed cuddling more than the others after their mother passed, perhaps because he was old enough to remember being in her loving arms. Not that the ones younger than he did not need her attention, he simply needed it more.

She doubted her father had taken time to make their morning meal, but who else could it be? The slant of the rising sun shining through the slot in her room let her know she had slept far too long. In a panic, she quickly got up, got dressed and was tying her belt when Wallace stuck his head in the door. "Come see, sister, 'tis a Viking breakfast."

Her mouth dropped. "A Viking is cooking?"

"Aye. He is an odd one, for he likes cooking."

"That is odd."

She finished tying her sword around her waist and followed her brother down the stairs. Wallace was right, Nikolas stood near the hearth stirring a big pot of porridge. All the children except the two youngest boys had gone outside, and Wallace had a knowing grin on his face when he walked out the door. She hesitantly took a seat at the table, another thing to which she was unaccustomed.

"Do you always sleep late, Catrina?" Nikolas asked.

She tipped her head to one side. "'Tis the first time in many months hungry children dinna wake me. Which one are you?"

Nikolas dipped a wooden bowl in the pot, wiped the excess mush off the side with a spoon and set it on the table for her. "I am the handsome one." He enjoyed her smile and then went back to stirring the porridge.

"Are you also the youngest?"

"Nay, I am third youngest. Almoor and Obbi are younger. How old are you?"

Catrina blushed. "I am but fourteen years."

"In our country, you are old enough to marry."

She ate a spoonful of porridge and savored the taste. "'Tis the same here, if a lass wishes it...which I do not."

He was shocked. "Not ever? At least six of my brothers shall find that greatly disappointing."

Katrina giggled. "Only six?"

"Of course, three are not yet old enough to marry." Nikolas used a cloth to protect his hand, lifted the pot out of the hearth, and carried it to the door. "I am Nikolas and I shall not tell my brothers you do not wish a husband. 'Twould spoil their morning meal." He grinned and then carried the pot out the door.

She waited until he was out of sight before she whispered, "He cooks?" Catrina dipped her spoon into the oats a second time. "Pity that one is too young. I might fancy him best."

"Me too," said Dughall. "Sister, why is he so big?"

She had almost forgotten her little brothers were listening to every word. "He is a Viking. All Vikings are big," Catrina answered. "You shall be big too when you are grown."

"And you shall be my wife," Dughall proudly announced.

When he picked up his bowl and chose the chair next to her, she gave him his morning hug. "I cannae, I am your sister."

Conan scrunched up his face. "I dinna want a wife. Wives are lassies."

Catrina giggled. "I am a lassie and you like me well enough."

As usual, little Conan had more porridge on his hands than in his mouth. Nevertheless, he put both hands on his hips. "You're not a lassie, you're a sister."

Catrina smiled, took another bite and again savored the taste of food she didn't have to cook for once. It tasted heavenly. She was still smiling when Kenna came in for her usual morning visit. "My prayers have been answered," she whispered. "He cooks!"

"Aye, they have no pot of their own to cook in, so your father said to use yours." Kenna took a seat across the table and lowered her voice too. "They arose early to wash the ocean salt out of their clothes."

"All of them?"

"I think 'twas all of them. Mother caught me watching and made me come away from the window. She says I must pay them no mind, but if I do not, Muriel will."

"Is she here this morning too?"

"Not that I saw, but I am expecting her at any moment."

Catrina shrugged and took another bite. "I doubt she even knows they are here."

"I doubt she could *not* know they are here. I wager every unmarried lass in all of Scotland knows they are here. We must make our choice hastily."

"You? Make a choice hastily? That I should like to see."

"You are right – they are all so very handsome, 'twill be impossible."

"What if none are old enough to marry?"

Kenna caught her breath. "Are they not all old enough?"

"You best ask them."

"I shall. I wonder what they are doing now?"

"Eating, would be my guess."

"Aye, eating. 'Tis a perfect time to ask them."

Catrina didn't think Kenna would take her seriously. "You mean to ask them outright? Can you not think of a better way?"

"Why *not* just ask them?"

Catrina leaned closer and whispered, "They might know you have lost your wits, if you do."

Kenna got up, went to the door, and paused just long enough to look back, "I cannae hide it forever anyway." She ignored Catrina's giggle, rushed out the door and disappeared.

*

It looked to be another sunny morning when Catrina finished her meal and stepped out the door to see what her brothers and sisters were doing. Beatan was sitting on the wall watching for Brodies. As was her particular chore, Elalsaid was feeding the chickens and checking on the newly laid eggs. Some eggs she left to hatch, while she collected others. Wallace and Niall were helping in the garden, and the little ones were with the next Viking to attract Catrina's particular attention.

To her amazement, Almoor sat on the ground in the middle of the courtyard with all the children facing him, not just her younger brothers and sisters. She was too far away to hear, but he appeared to be telling them a story. Just learning how to walk, even the youngest member of the clan was there and Almoor had her seated in his lap with two other little ones on each knee. It made Catrina smile. When she looked, two of the mothers stood in their cottage doorways smiling also. Seldom did they get a moment of relief from raising children.

The men were working in the garden, save the other six brothers who appeared to be at their leisure. Two of them were back in the water, one was climbing up to sit atop the wall with Beaton, and the others, including Karr, were nowhere in sight. She hardly noticed it when Kenna walked up beside her.

"Your father forbade them to work this day, for they need their strength to fight the Brodies," Kenna said.

Catrina looked up the garden hill at her father, "Yet, he does not rest."

"True, I have never seen him take but the time needed to eat and drink. The other lads do, but not him. Why does he do it?"

"Perhaps he shall, now that we have more help." Catrina turned her attention back to the children.

"He teaches them courage," Kenna muttered, nodding in Almoor's direction. "Pity he is too young to marry, for I should fancy him if he were not."

"You asked them?"

"Aye, the eldest is twenty and three, and the youngest is fourteen." Kenna sighed. "I am forced to choose from only the elder four."

"I cannae think how you shall manage."

Kenna started to twist her hair again. "I know, I am quite put out about it."

"Have you forgotten Donahue, Garth, and Grant?"

Kenna looked sideways at her friend. "I have not forgotten, but still they do not speak up. I gladly mark them off my board."

"You have a board?"

"Not yet, but I am thinking of making one. How else can I see which of them smiles at me most often?" Kenna knew better, but when she glanced at her cottage, her mother was standing in the doorway waving her over. "What could she possibly want now?"

Catrina watched her hurry home and then considered the brothers again. Nikolas cooked, Almoor loved children, and she wondered if any of the others had something she might admire. If she was not interested in one or two of the brothers for herself, perhaps she might be able to give her sister sound advice. After all, Elalsaid would be old enough to marry in a year or two – if she ever grew out of her propensity to daydream.

She oddly found herself looking for Karr, and surprised herself in doing so. Instead, she spotted Hani and watched him for a time. He seemed most interested in examining the vegetation and the land. Twice he knelt down, picked up a handful of dirt and let it slide through his fingers. He seemed as pleasant as the other brothers, but he was the one who had yet to smile.

Before long, she spotted Steinn talking to Grant near the foot of the garden. From what she could hear, Steinn wanted to compare Scotland's growing methods to those in his own country. They decided the basic difference was the length of the growing season. She was still watching and listening when she heard her father call her name.

"Catrina?"

She looked up the hill, saw him motion for her to come and started up. Careful not to trample the newly turned soil, she took the side path and made her way past the other men to the top. "Aye, Father?"

He laid down his shovel, took her hand and led her away from the others. "You shall find favor in the eyes of the brothers, but take care, daughter. They shall be tempted to fight for you and we need them to fight the Brodies."

She deeply wrinkled his brow. "Fight for me? Surely not, they are brothers."

"'Tis possible, I have seen such a thing before."

"But Father, how shall I prevent it?"

"Watch them not, leastwise where they can see and give no more attention to one than the others. Until you choose a husband, you must carefully consider how they shall see what you do."

His caution gave her the perfect opening. "Suppose I dinna choose any of them in the end?"

"You favor Grant? I have seen how you look at him."

"'Tis true, I did once, but I have grown up." She enjoyed her father's smile before she continued. "I think he favors Kenna."

"I see."

"When the time comes, which I hope shall not be too soon, will you help me choose a husband?"

"Nay, daughter. This, you must do alone."

"And will you take a wife?"

Her question took him aback. "I am too old to take another wife."

Catrina giggled. "If I take a husband, you shall need a wife to care for all your children." With a grin on her face, she started back down the hill.

Stefan frowned. He watched her walk back to the castle, and then glanced at the other MacGreagor women going about their daily chores. He preferred neither of the two who had lost their husbands, shook his head and went back to work. Yet, the seed had been planted. What would he do if Catrina married?

*

Once Catrina spotted Karr finally, she tried not to pay attention to any of the Vikings, but nothing kept Kenna from pointing out a different one every chance she got. Therefore, as the two of them carried buckets of fresh water to the castle and to each of the cottages, she found herself watching them anyway. It was not their usual chore, it was Kenna's idea, and she insisted they pause regularly to watch the men. At least the other women were grateful, though a little suspicious.

The three youngest brothers, Nikolas, Almoor and Obbi, were constantly bickering with each other, and Catrina had to admit they were fun to watch. She supposed, since none were of marrying age, watching them would do no real harm. Just now, they were trying to prove which was the strongest by carrying large rocks to the stonewall. Nikolas held his rock out, threatening to drop it on Obbi's foot, and made Catrina laugh.

"Did your father not tell them to rest?" Kenna asked.

"So you said." She glanced up the hill and noticed both Steinn and Karr were helping in the garden. Magnus was mixing mortar for the wall, and Hani had an axe and was heading into the woods. "I dinna think they know how to rest."

\*

With chores to do inside, Catrina didn't come back outside until past noon. She was surprised to see her father sitting on the log with the brothers. When each of the brothers looked at her, she quickly looked away and went to find Kenna. She felt as if every eye was on her and had she looked back, she would have known she was right. She didn't look back. Catrina was relieved when Kenna came out of her cottage to join her.

"They watch us," Catrina whispered.

"And they smile, save the strange one. Is it not grand?"

She started them walking down the path beside the loch. "Not always. Perhaps when they become more accustomed to us, they shall stop."

"I hope they never stop," Kenna sighed. "I wonder what your father is saying to them?"

"So do I." Catrina tugged on Kenna's arm, led her through the trees and then stood in the woods behind the brothers and her father.

"Lads," Stefan was saying, "we are in need of hunters. Which of you are the best?" He was surprised when none of them answered. "You know not how to hunt?" he asked.

"We are better at fishing," Karr answered. "What do you hunt for in Scotland?"

"Wild boar, deer, bear, and rabbit. Bears and wild boar are the most dangerous."

"We can build ships," said Hani.

"We hardly have need of ships. Can ye build cottages?" Stefan asked.

"Aye," Karr answered, "and we can teach the lads how to fight like Vikings."

"Can you fix a roof?" Stefan asked.

"Aye, that we can do," Hani answered.

Stefan looked at the vegetable garden and wondered if they could ever grow enough to feed everyone. "But ye cannae hunt."

"We can learn," Almoor put in.

"Or we can barter for food," Magnus suggested.

"Barter with what? I have used all the coins my father gave me," said Stefan.

Karr got up and went into his cottage. He noticed Kenna and Catrina in the woods watching, but he ignored them. When he came back, he was holding the odd sack that rattled. He opened it and let Stefan see the coins and the other gold and silver items inside. "'Tis Anundi's plunder. 'Twill be enough?" Karr asked.

Stefan raised both eyebrows. "Aye, more than enough. We can barter with the Macorans and the Limonds for what we need, then." He took a deep relaxed breath. "Perhaps we shall see Ronan fight to be laird of the Macoran's this afternoon, if they have not already fought." He looked toward the nearest Macoran farm and decided they would have heard if the fight was finished.

All seven of the brothers smiled, all except Hani, of course.

"First, I wish you to fix the roof," said Stefan.

"Which one?" Almoor asked, glancing at all the cottages. What he could see of the other roofs looked fine to him.

Stefan pointed toward the castle. "That one."

"Ah," said Almoor.

All seven of them stared at the height of the three-story building, but none of them made a move.

"Three," Karr finally guessed.

"Or four," said Magnus. "We have never tried four."

Karr stood up and with the others following, walked to the structure to get a closer look. "Aye, four," he said.

Perplexed, Stefan drew closer and frowned. "Four what?"

"Four brothers," Karr answered.

"I get the top," Obbi shouted, drawing the attention of the whole clan.

"You always get the top," Nikolas loudly complained.

Catrina and Kenna gave up their hiding place and moved closer. Everyone else was watching, so Catrina didn't see any harm in watching too. Besides, none of the brothers were paying any attention to her.

"I am the lightest, is why," Obbi argued. He waited for the brothers to gather and then stiffened his body so Karr and Magnus could hoist him atop Almoor's shoulders. Next, Almoor stiffened his body and the brother's lifted the two of them until they could plant Almoor's feet on Steinn's shoulders. Still, the brothers were not high enough to reach the top.

Karr stood back and surveyed the distance. "Aye, four."

"Four?" Steinn groaned. The wait of his brothers seemed to have increased since the last time they tried their balancing act.

Stefan could not help but smile. "We've stair steps in the back."

"What?" Steinn gasped. He abruptly turned to look at Stefan, and when he did, Obbi began to lose his balance. He started to sway and flail his arms. Beneath him, Almoor couldn't keep his balance either. He let go of Obbi's legs, felt his brother jump off, and then he too jumped down, rolling as he landed.

Almoor sat up and stared at Stefan. "You might have said that in the beginning."

The crowd roared with laughter and Catrina rolled her eyes. "They cannae hunt, but they can entertain us," she whispered to Kenna.

"Aye, and such handsome entertainers." Kenna watched all the brothers walk around to the back of the castle, and in a few moments, two of them appeared on the roof. "I fancy the second one," Kenna said.

"Magnus?"

"Is that his name? I fancy his name too." She dreamily repeated it, "Magnus."

"Kenna, you are hopeless. Suppose he snores or dibbles food down his front when he eats. Suppose he laughs at that which is not funny, and frowns at that which is? Suppose he…"

"Very well, I shall wait a day or two more to decide. I suppose we shall be forced to listen outside their cottage doors to learn which one snores."

"With four in one cottage and three in the other, how shall we know which it is?"

"You are right. We shall ask them."

Catrina patted the top of Kenna's head and then went home. The brothers had been MacGreagors for scant few hours and already she knew she liked each of them. Not only that, she fancied one more than the others. It was time to admit it, if only to herself. On the other hand, she hardly knew him and she heeded her father's warnings well; do not look at him often, do not abide promises or threats, and – do not dream of him constantly. She made the last one up herself, for that seemed to be an increasing problem. Even now, she was standing in front of one of the slots watching him.

She puffed her cheeks and went to see how much dried meat she had left to put in the evening stew. It normally took half a day of cooking at least to soften it up so the little ones could chew it. They certainly could use more hunters. Hopefully, the brothers could learn how to sneak up on their prey and quickly.

*

Muriel could not wait to tell Catrina the news, even if she had to face Kenna's accusations to do it. Rumors about Ronan's particular predicament had spread quickly and with her father's permission, she wanted to be the first to tell the MacGreagors. Boldly, she walked down the path, crossed the courtyard, peeked in the open door, and entered the castle.

"Catrina, I have such a story to tell."

"Muriel, I am happy to see you." As soon as Muriel came in, Catrina walked to the door, just to see where Kenna was. She was nowhere in sight, but as soon as she heard, Kenna was sure to come. "'Tis not bad news, I hope."

"'Tis bad news for Ronan." Muriel's curly red hair was just as unruly as it always was, but it suited her and her green eyes glistened with delight. "He has gone hard of hearing."

"Truly?" Catrina asked. She poured two goblets of very weak ale and joined Muriel at the table.

"He awoke this morning with a fierce headache. 'Tis no wonder after the handsome Viking threw him against the tree. But after, when he awoke, I mean, he drank wine to cure his head and plenty of it."

"He drank himself sillier than he normally is?"

Muriel laughed out loud. "Aye, he was found passed out with his head laid flat on Laird Macoran's table."

"Is he passed out still?"

"Nay, for that is how we know he cannae hear. The clan has chosen Davie to be our laird, and when Davie went to challenge him, Ronan could not hear a word…that is, once they managed to awaken him. First, he yawned to try to clear the fog in his ears. When that didn't work, Ronan tipped his head to one side and pounded the other ear with his hand. Still, he could not hear, so he pounded the other ear. It was then he opened his eyes and realized three Macorans were staring at him."

"How I would have liked seeing that," said Catrina.

"Davie tried talking, but to no avail. He had to yell his challenge loudly three times. He yelled so loud he was heard outside." She laughed again. "Still, Ronan dinna hear him. Our brave Ronan put a finger in each ear, furiously wiggled them around, but that dinna help either."

"I cannae imagine not being able to hear, but I must say I am not that sorry for him."

"Nor is anyone else, save Davie. 'Tis why they shall race instead."

"Race instead of fight?" Catrina asked.

"Who means to fight?" Kenna interrupted, sticking her head in the door, and then inviting herself in. She chose a chair directly across the table from Muriel. "Quite far from home, are you not?"

Muriel glared, "Have you lost your broom?"

Kenna narrowed her eyes too. "You needed running off that day. I know you have set your sights on Grant."

"Have I? 'Tis news to me." Muriel shot back.

"I dinna believe a word you say. 'Tis…"

"Kenna," Catrina interrupted, "there is news of Ronan. He has gone hard of hearing."

Kenna's eyes lit up. "Has he?"

"As I was telling," said Muriel, turning back to Catrina, "Ronan tried pounding on first one ear and then the other to unplug them. When that dinna work, he shoved a finger in each and wiggled. Davie saw no blood on Ronan's fingers."

"Davie?" Kenna asked. "What has Davie to do with it?"

Muriel took an exasperated breath. "The clan has chosen Davie to lead us – and dinna pretend you were not listening outside the door this whole time. I saw your shadow."

Kenna was caught and she knew it. She shifted her eyes from side to side, trying to think of a way out, and was grateful when Catrina asked another question.

"Why are they to race instead of fight, though? Ronan has not lost his sight as well, has he?"

"Nay, he can see well enough. 'Tis that Davie thinks it unfair to fight a lad who cannae hear. 'Twould belittle the clan and everyone agrees."

"Ronan rides a horse well enough," said Catrina. "He quickly rides away when I threaten to tell Father he is here."

Muriel laughed. "They say when Ronan finally understood; he laid his head back down on the table and went to sleep."

"Do they wait for him to wake again?" Kenna asked in a much more gentle tone.

Muriel was not fooled. Kenna would have a sassy remark no matter what answer she gave, so she didn't answer. "The clansmen are already placing their wagers."

"For or against Ronan?" Catrina asked.

"No one wants him to win," Muriel confessed, "but he can ride a horse as well as any lad."

"Confess it, you fancy Grant," Kenna abruptly accused.

Muriel grinned. "Perhaps I did, but that was before the Vikings came." She ignored the furious look on Kenna's face and addressed Catrina again. "They are the most handsome lads in the whole world. What might be their names?"

"They are taken," Kenna grumbled.

"Already? Whom have they asked to marry?"

Catrina was incredulous. "Aye, Kenna, taken by who?"

Kenna rubbed the end of her itchy nose trying to buy herself time to think of something. "Well…they soon will be."

Catrina ignored her and turned to Muriel. "The four eldest are Karr, Steinn, Magnus and…"

"Hani," Kenna added. "Come to think of it, Hani would be perfect for you. He has yet to smile, and married to you, he would have no cause to smile anyway."

"She fancies Hani?" Muriel asked Catrina, "I see, she thinks to turn me against him, but the lad who chooses her is not the lad for me anyway."

"I do *not* fancy Hani," Kenna snapped. "I fancy the tallest, for he is the most handsome of them all."

Catrina felt a sudden and odd surge of jealousy. It surprised her. "I suppose he is the most handsome."

"'Twould do you no good if he is," said Kenna. "You wish not to marry for years and years to come."

"Years?" Muriel asked. "I can hardly wait another month or two." She stood up and once more glared at Kenna. "I thank you for the ale, Catrina, but I must go home where I am truly welcome."

"The path is that way," said Kenna, pointing out the door.

As soon as she was gone, Catrina shook her head. "You are very unkind to her. She has truly never wronged either of us. 'Tis only that you fear she shall take the lad you finally decide you want."

"Aye and she will too." Kenna cringed when she heard her mother calling. "Not again," she muttered as she too headed out the door.

Catrina could not contain her curiosity. She went to the door to see where Karr was and if he was watching either Muriel of Kenna. He was not. Instead, he was hard at work, carrying rocks to the wall while two of his brothers worked with him. Grant was watching Muriel, however, which was certain to displease Kenna, but it made Catrina smile. It appeared Grant had made his choice after all.

As if he knew right where she was, Karr picked up a rock, paused, and looked at her. He did not smile, but his eyes met hers just the way they did before he got off the ship. This time, it made her heart skip a beat, so she abruptly went back inside. There was a broom to make and she best get to it, before other chores demanded her attention. Still, while she gathered the heather sprigs around the end of her broom handle and tightly wrapped the twine around it, she paused several times to consider the strange excitement he caused. Soon, she convinced herself it was all her imagination.

# CHAPTER 8

There simply wasn't enough time for Catrina to tell her father what Muriel said about Ronan. Conan fell down, skinned his knee and needed her attention. Garbhan came running in for his hug and Aileen broke the head off her doll. A little water and mortar would fix that, of course, but by then, Karr, Steinn, Magnus, Hani, and Stefan, had ridden away. Catrina shrugged and went to dip the broken neck of doll head in the mortar bucket.

*

It didn't take long for the brothers to patch the roof with enough thatching to see that it didn't leak again for quite some time. At least they hoped so. The three youngest, Nikolas, Almoor, and Obbi, were excited to go on the hunt with Grant, who was more than willing to take them. Hopefully, they could bring back enough fresh meat to feed the clan for a day or two, at least. Grant waited until they gathered their bows and arrows, and then led them up the side of the hill to the vast forests north of the village.

*

"We normally barter for wheat and oats from the Limonds," Stefan explained on the way to the Macoran village, "but buying from the Macoran's might yield more than what we need to survive."

With coins from Anundi's sack in a pouch tucked in his belt, Karr rode beside Stefan, and once more looked over the rich farmland. Before long, he could also see the river on the other side. "You mean, it might better secure an alliance?"

"Aye. Laird Limond is a good lad like his uncle before him. The Limonds and the Macorans once fought over the salmon in the river, for they each bartered them to the English. Now, the two clans work together."

"Will that end if Ronan is the Macoran laird?"

"I cannae imagine the Macoran's would make Ronan their laird, but if they do..." They were halfway there when Stefan called a halt.

"What is it?" Karr asked.

"The farmers are not in the fields; their hearths have little smoke, and only a few children play."

The brothers took a long look around. Stefan was right.

"Follow me," he said, turning up the path that led to the top of the hill. From there, they could see both the village and the ocean below without being detected. As soon as they reached the top, they stopped and got off their horses. They could hear distant voices, but not the shouts expected when men were preparing to fight. With Stefan leading the way, they made their way through the trees until they had a good view of the village below. The Macorans were gathered in the courtyard, but oddly, none of the men looked like they were preparing to fight. Instead, they appeared to be looking at something up the beach. Stefan motioned for them to follow and moved to a place where they could see the water's edge all the way from the graveyard to the beginning of the village. Not far from the graveyard, two men sat on horses staring at a third man, who had his sword in the air preparing to signal the beginning of the race.

"They race?" asked Karr. He recognized the silly one he threw against the tree, but he didn't remember the other.

Stefan gasped, "I dinna believe it. They race instead of fight."

"Who might the other one be?" Hani asked.

"He is Davie," Stefan asked. "He is a good rider, but so is Ronan. I have seen them race before. If Ronan wins..."

Before Stefan could finish his sentence, the third man swiftly sliced his sword through the air, and the race began.

Davie's horse bolted and clearly took the lead, but not for long. Ronan, not to be outdone and with the most to lose, slapped the back of his horse with the straps to his reins and soon caught up. For a moment, they were neck and neck, as both horses shot toward the finish line drawn in the dirt.

It was a dead heat, until – a man began to repeatedly beat the Macoran gong.

"Vikings," Stefan gasped. For only a split second, he stopped watching the race and looked to the horizon. Sure enough, two longship sails were just beginning to appear.

Unfortunately, the ships caught Davie's attention too and when he looked, his horse slowed. His pause lasted just long enough for Ronan to pull ahead. Too late, Davie kicked the side of his horse and tried to catch up, but it was useless. By the time he reached the finish line, his horse was a full head behind Ronan's.

"Noooo," Stefan moaned. Bitterly disappointed, he shook his head. "It cannae be."

*

In the courtyard, Ronan expected to see the people cheering. They weren't and when he glanced around, several of the men had drawn their swords. Afraid he was about to be cut down, he thought to keep right on going. So he did.

That is, until he reached the edge of the village, looked behind him, and discovered he was not being chased. He halted, turned his horse around, and realized what was happening. The people were once more running to hide their children and gather their arms for battle. "Vikings!" he shouted. He was now their legitimate laird, after all, and it was his duty to shout commands.

Nevertheless, his hearing was so bad, he could hardly hear his own voice and it did not appear anyone else did either. "Light the fire!" His voice still sounded muddled and he was clearly being ignored. He touched his throat just to make certain he still had one, and then jumped down off his horse and ran back to the courtyard.

In a panic, he flew up the steps, crossed the walkway and yanked open the door. Inside the Keep, he grabbed his weapons and lifted the helmet off the table, but then he put it back. They weren't going to throw him against a tree again – not now that he was the true Macoran laird. The lads were duty bound to protect him this time.

Ronan slowly drew his sword, puffed his chest and stepped out on the walkway of *his* Keep.

*

"They look for us," Karr whispered, standing beside Stefan on the hill.

"Aye," Hani agreed, "they are the two we left on the waterfront. 'Tis good we burned the ship."

"How did they know to look for us here?" Magnus wondered.

"I dinna know," answered Karr. "We told no one where we were going."

"They came so soon," Steinn muttered. Careful to stay hidden, he moved to stand behind another tree so he could get a better view. "'Tis possible they saw us from behind and guessed where we were going."

"We saw nothing of them and we kept careful watch," said Hani.

Karr rubbed the back of his neck. "They could not have been very far behind."

Not once had Stefan's eyes left the ships. "They have stopped and I see no others."

Steinn nodded. "'Tis doubtful they come just to kill us, they search for their ship."

"*Their* ship? Did you not say you were ship builders?"

"We were," Steinn answered. "We built them, but we were not given one to sail."

Stefan was incredulous. "You stole the ship?"

"The King would not have allowed it, so we neglected to ask," Karr admitted.

Stefan couldn't help but grin. "I must hear this story when we get home. I dinna think 'twas possible to steal a longship."

"'Tis not possible," said Magnus, "lest you've lost your wits. We knew not how to sail it and nearly sank it twice."

"Three times," Hani corrected. "You forget the sea monsters."

Stefan's eyes widened. "You saw them?"

"Aye, they are black and white, and nearly as big as any ship we have ever seen. Had they not left us be, I thought to give them Hani," said Steinn.

At that, Stefan nearly laughed out loud. "Those are whales. Have you never seen a whale?"

"We have seen white ones, but none the size of those," Magnus answered.

When Stefan looked back at the Viking ships, he began to worry. The men still had their oars in the water and it looked as though they were preparing to attack. A few minutes later, the first ship turned south and then made ready to hoist the sail again. The other ship soon followed and everyone on the hilltop, in the Macoran Village, and in the Limond village, took a relieved breath.

In the Macoran courtyard, Ronan stood proudly on the wooden walkway just above the steps. The people had just begun to relax and put their weapons away when they realized what had happened. Ashamed of himself, Davie hung his head and left the village. In shocked silence, the Macorans stared in wonderment at the man they were now forced to follow.

"Why do they not just kill him," Karr asked as the brothers and Stefan mounted their horses and started down the hill.

"'Tis not their way to kill a lad, save in a fair fight," Stefan answered, as he led them down the beach to the courtyard.

As soon as he saw the MacGreagors, Ronan smirked. "Have you brought me your daughter, MacGreagor?"

Hani gritted his teeth. "Let me kill him."

"Nay," Stefan countered. He narrowed his eyes, glared at the Macoran's new laird, and then ignored him and turned to the people. "We come to barter for horses and food. Who is willing to pledge enough wheat to see us through winter?"

One of the men asked, "What have you to barter?"

"If you agree, I shall show you," said Stefan.

"What is he saying?" Ronan demanded. No one answered, at least not that he could tell.

"And if the crops fail?" another man shouted.

"Then you shall pay us the year following. I pray they do not fail, for if they do, we shall all have to barter with the English." Stefan looked at several other men who seemed to be interested.

"I demand someone tell me what he is saying," Ronan bellowed.

Alton let out an exasperated breath and climbed the steps to the walkway. He leaned close to Ronan's ear and yelled, "They wish to barter for our crops!"

Ronan was furious and glared at Alton. "The Macoran's do not barter with the MacGreagors – not until they give me Catrina."

Stefan was just beginning to catch on. "He has lost his hearing?" he asked.

"Aye," Alton nodded.

"A blatherskite with no hearing?" Stefan asked with a grin.

"What did he say?" Ronan demanded.

"He said," Alton yelled, "you cannae have his daughter."

"Then he cannae have our food," Ronan shot back.

"Very well," said Stefan, "we shall get what we need from the Limonds." Just as he started to turn his horse, a farmer shouted.

"You can barter with me, MacGreagor."

Stefan intentionally turned his back on Ronan and raised his hand. "Let no blood be shed on our account. Yet, if you manage to rid yourself of the laddie, you know where to find us." With that, he led the Vikings through the village and down the path toward home.

"Poison," Magnus said when they were well away.

"I agree," said Hani and Steinn at the same time.

Stefan shook his head. "Let the lads in his clan kill him. 'Tis the only way. If we kill him, the Macorans will turn on us."

"But he demands Catrina," Karr said. "Will he try to take her?"

Stefan gave that careful consideration. "Aye, if he dares. He would have to fight me if he did, and he cowers at the sight of me. Yet, if he marries one of Laird Brodie's daughters, as unsightly as some fancy they are, we shall have enemies on both sides of us."

"I will see these Brodie daughters," said Steinn. He may have been frightened of the monsters in the sea, but there wasn't a man alive he feared.

Stefan turned in his seat on his horse to look back. "Nay, you shall not. If you are caught, they shall sell you into slavery and we cannae afford the time to rescue you."

Steinn boldly boasted, "They shall not capture me."

Stefan rolled his eyes. "I thought the same. How old are you, lad?"

"I am nineteen years."

He was about to say something more when he heard the pounding of horse's hooves behind him. Stefan led the Vikings into the trees to wait and watch. He expected it to be Ronan and a full guard. Instead, several farmers appeared. He walked his horse back to the path and waited until they slowed and stopped.

"We wish to sell our crops and our horses, MacGreagor," said the first.

"Against Ronan's command?"

"If none tell, he shall never know."

"Very well," Stefan said. "Come to the village and we shall set the barter. The lads need a pot to cook in, if you can spare one. Bring whatever you no longer need and we shall pay you. Agreed?"

Smiling, each of them nodded, turned their horses and rode away.

"'Tis at least a few lads with their wits about them," Karr said as the brothers came out of the trees to join Stefan.

"Aye. They shall find a way to rid themselves of Ronan soon enough."

Karr couldn't get Ronan's threat out of his mind, and he wondered just how hard it would be to sneak into the Macoran Keep one night, and end Ronan's threat with a sword. Probably not hard, for he had often practiced being quiet. In fact, he could walk through a forest without alarming the animals. What worried him was that Ronan would carry Catrina off, and he wasn't about to let that happen. It was not the first time he had dealt with men obsessed with power, wealth and having the woman they desired. More often than not, men like that would not relent until they were dead…a possibility that suited Karr just fine.

\*

Grant MacGreagor was a reasonable man who assumed all men knew how to keep from getting lost. It didn't take long for the Vikings to lose their sense of direction, however, especially since they could not easily see the placement of sun in the unfamiliar forest.

At least the Vikings knew how to walk through the woods without scaring the prey away, although Obbi was a bit more awkward than his older brothers. Just coming out of the difficult age of fourteen, and with Nikolas constantly laughing at him, he didn't mind lingering behind a little. Besides, he had yet to be the better marksman.

At last, they saw a red deer nibbling grass near a stream and Grant nodded for Almoor to take the first shot. Almoor missed, but Nikolas didn't, and when the arrow brought the animal quickly down, their shouts of joy should have told Obbi where the others were, but when they looked, he was nowhere in sight.

"He is lost," Almoor muttered.

"I dinna recall anyone ever getting lost in these woods before," Grant pondered.

"He is rattlebrained," Nikolas announced.

"He is not," Almoor argued. "Not usually." He turned, cupped his hands and shouted, "Obbi!" Suddenly, Grant grasped his shoulder from behind. "What?"

"Brodies."

Almoor's eyes widened. "Do you think they captured him?"

"I hope not, but we best not let the Brodies know where we are."

Almoor nodded. He helped Grant hoist the deer onto Nikolas's shoulders and then followed as Grant took them back the way they came.

It wasn't long before they found Obbi, sitting on a log with his bow loaded and his arrow pointed at a rabbit burrow. The burrow was nearly hidden behind a bush, and the rabbit was nowhere in sight.

"I say we stay and watch," Nikolas said, moving the deer a little higher on his shoulders. "The rabbit shall outwit him, which is easily done."

"If you keep talking, it will," Obbi disgustedly said without taking his eyes off the burrow.

Grant smiled. He was starting to like the brothers a lot, especially Nikolas. "How is it you speak our language?"

"Stefan's aunt taught us. She and her sister were snatched away from the Limonds by his father."

"I dinna know that. My father served as a slave with Stefan, but he dinna make it past two years after we became MacGreagors."

"Our father died too," Almoor volunteered. "Have you a mother?"

"Aye, she is Sarah. She is…"

Exasperated, Obbi finally lowered his arrow and stood up. "Fine hunters you are. 'Tis a perfectly good rabbit and 'tis now lost to us." He turned his back on the others and started toward home.

"Have you not noticed? We shot a deer," Nikolas bragged. "'Tis far better than a stupid rabbit."

Obbi huffed and took long, noisy strides through the woods. "Try putting deer in rabbit stew, then."

"Rabbit stew…deer stew, what be the difference?" Nikolas persisted.

"The rabbit!" Obbi shouted back.

Behind them, the rabbit peeked out of the burrow, decided it was safe, and hopped away.

*

When they returned home, Stefan informed the men and word of the new Macoran laird spread quickly. The work in the vegetable garden was done for the day and the men were working on the stonewall, so the brothers went back to work as well. Everyone was pleased when the hunters brought back their gain. The deer had been hung from the limb of a tree until time to skin it. After that, it would be cut up and divided among the clan's households. Stefan's sons were still taking turns sitting on the wall and watching for Brodies, while the little ones played and the women went about their usual chores.

Karr looked for her, but when he didn't see Catrina, he became concerned. That is, until he decided Ronan couldn't possibly have gotten there ahead of them. Even so, he scanned the trees on the hillside above the garden. Satisfied Ronan was not there, he went back to carrying rocks and wondering how he would ever get her to marry him. It looked like Nikolas managed to impress her. She could not say enough about his willingness to cook. She had already thanked him several times just for one meal.

She seemed pleased with Almoor's way with children too, but Karr couldn't think of one single talent he had that might attract her attention. In fact, he was certain he didn't have one, and the worry lines steadily grew deeper in his forehead. When she finally came out of the castle, he saw her climb to the top of the hill with Kenna and then disappeared into the forest. He set his rock down and began to follow. When he looked, Stefan was watching him and it was apparent he was thinking the same thing. Stefan nodded, giving Karr permission to watch over them, and soon he walked into the thickness of the forest.

*

They planned to go up the hill to see if the wild berries were ripe yet anyway, and now was as good a time for them to talk where others could not hear. "Have you heard? Ronan won and 'tis he who is the new laird," Kenna said.

Catrina stopped walking and stared at her friend. "Impossible, the Macoran's have more wits than that."

"Nevertheless, they have done it."

Catrina deeply sighed and then continued walking. "At grandfather's burying, Ronan asked for me...rather he offered to make a trade. He would let father have Anundi's sword for me."

"How brash of him. What did Stefan do?"

"He said he would not trade me for all the Macoran land and everything it in."

"I knew he would not agree. Did Ronan keep the sword?"

"Nay, Father took it anyway. No finer sword have I ever seen. 'Tis in the castle if you wish to see it."

"Perhaps later. I am not fond of swords, as you are well aware, not even the very fine ones. I pray for the day lads shall fight no more."

"As do we all." Catrina wound her way through the trees and bushes until she came to the first raspberry bush. "Oh, Kenna, what shall I do? Ronan said if he could not have me, he would make an alliance with the Brodies and let them attack us."

"You dinna agree to marry him, did you?"

"Of course not, I'd rather marry a Brodie – and I would surely die if I was put upon to do that."

Kenna walked around to the other side of the bush, pulled a green raspberry off its stem and examined it. "Laird Brodie's son was not *that* unsightly."

Catrina once more stared at her best friend. "You have gone daft, finally. Never have I seen a lad so...so unworthy. His hair is black, his nose is an odd shape and his eyes are too far apart."

"Are they? I had not noticed that." Kenna bit her lip, thought about it and then grinned. "You are jesting. Besides, you see the bad in all lads."

"And you see only the good? A look, a smile, the slightest tribute, and you are in love beyond measure."

"Admit it, you like a tribute as much as I."

Finding only green berries, Catrina moved to another bush. "They are but idle words. Your father calls your mother his bonnie lass all the time."

"My mother *is* Bonnie."

"Of course she is, but he says it so often, I wonder that she does not tire of it."

"It makes her smile each time, so I dinna think she shall ever tire of it."

"Well, I dinna wish to hear it...ever. Rupert says it to his wife when he wants her to do something, and she is wise enough to know it. I have seen the crossness in her eyes, and I should hate a lad who treated me thusly so."

Kenna tossed that raspberry away and moved to the next bush as well. Some of the berries were starting to turn slightly pink, but red was weeks away. "Aye, but if a handsome lad..."

"You think them all handsome. Aside from how handsome they are, what good do you see in any of them?"

"Well…"

Catrina put her hands on her hips. "Go on."

"I cannae, I've a sudden headache." Kenna grabbed her head with both hands.

Catrina laughed. "I can see why. Thinking always gives you a headache."

"Your grandfather married a Brodie to keep them from attacking the Macorans, you know."

That surprised Catrina. "He dinna, did he?"

"'Tis what my father said. The Brodies were about to kill all the Macorans when Laird Macoran made the offer. Later, he set her aside and married your grandmother."

"I see. I wonder why no one has told that story before?"

"Perhaps it dinna matter before."

"But now it does? You are saying I should be as gallant as my grandfather, and marry Ronan to save the MacGreagors."

"Let it not come to that, dear friend, but if it does, marrying Ronan would be better than being wed to a Brodie…unless 'tis Laird Brodie's handsome son."

Catrina rolled her eyes. "I've a better idea. *You* marry a Brodie to save the clan."

Kenna lifted her chin. "I cannae. You know very well Father would never allow it. He hates the Brodies."

"Then we have no choice – we must make a run for it."

"'Twould never work, Mother would call and I would be forced to come back."

"You are right. I must stay as well. Who better than I to make Conan brave finally, if making Conan brave is indeed possible."

Kenna whimsically looked at the drifting clouds in the sky. "Perhaps 'twould not be too awfully bad if Ronan was to marry a Brodie. We would still have an alliance with the Limonds, and to form an alliance with the Brodies, he must marry one of Laird Brodie's daughters. I have heard they are quite unsightly. Would it not serve Ronan right to have an unsightly wife?"

Catrina had not thought of that. "It would indeed."

"Have you seen them?"

"Of course not, you know we are forbidden to go anywhere near a Brodie."

"Grant might know. I have heard him say that when he goes hunting, he sometimes sees Brodies. I shall ask him if he has seen the daughters."

"Please do."

At the distant sound of her mother's voice, Kenna puffed her cheeks. "What could she possibly want now?"

"You best go. There are few berries ripe enough yet anyway." She watched her friend go back over the top of the hill and when Kenna was far enough away, she turned to look into the forest. "'You may show yourself now."

Karr was shocked. He didn't think he had ever walked through the trees more quietly. Even so, he was caught, and there was nothing he could do but step out from behind the bushes. "How did you know?"

"I have excellent hearing. Why are you watching us?"

"I...your father is worried Ronan might try to snatch you away."

"I see. I must take better care to see he does not."

"Aye, you must."

She nodded and started to go home. "Catrina, you need not marry him."

It was the first time he said her name, and she liked the sound of it. What she didn't like was that he heard every word they said. She looked down and tried to avoid his piercing eyes. "'Tis the way of Scotland. For every lad who is forced, there are likely a hundred lasses married off to see the clans live in peace. If I am asked, I too shall do it."

"Your father will never allow it."

"My father is very wise. If he deems it necessary, he shall allow it." With that, she turned and walked away.

Behind her, Karr couldn't remember a time he felt so inept. His chance to impress her had come and gone, with far less than favorable results. If anything, she seemed annoyed. Winning her was going to be a lot more difficult than he imagined, especially now that she had actually considered marrying the simpleton, Ronan Macoran. She loved her people, and for that he admired her, but if he died trying, he would somehow make her love him even more.

*

Ronan was not the only one who liked to watch the MacGreagors. A long time ago, Branan Brodie discovered a place between three bushes that kept him completely covered, and still afforded him a good view of the MacGreagor village. He was pretty sure he knew nearly everything about them, especially the one they called, Kenna. She caught his eye from the very beginning, and even though she was sometimes trivial, he liked her easy manner and the sound of her laughter. Life with her would be anything but boring.

When he first saw her, Kenna was not yet old enough, and he was content to wait for her to grow up, although it had not been without some measure of distress. More than once, his father accused him of being too backward to marry, but Branan cared not what that old goat said.

Rare were the times she and Catrina came close enough for him to hear what was said. This was one of those times, and he was more than pleased to hear she fancied him too. He also saw Karr and kept perfectly still praying the largest of the newly arrived giants would not discover him. Thankfully, he was not discovered, and as soon as all of them were gone, he slowly stood up.

The problems surrounding taking Kenna to be his wife were almost insurmountable, but now he had another problem. Until now, Ronan was just a bumbling half-wit, easily caught when he too tried to watch the MacGreagors. Yet, if what Catrina said was true, his beloved sisters were about to become barter in the centuries old game of clan alliances.

Something had to be done – and soon. He crept through the trees, found his horse, and rode off to find a Macoran hunter.

# CHAPTER 9

The MacGreagors expected to see the Macoran farmers early the next morning, perhaps as soon as when they first got up, but it was after the noon meal before they arrived. Even then, they came through the trees instead of down the path. The men tied their horses at the edge of the woods, walked the rest of the way and were relieved when Stefan and Karr took them inside the castle. Two of them carried full sacks and set them on the table.

Glad for the break in her chores, Catrina nodded to the last man to enter, and then went outside to ask Kenna why they had come. Kenna didn't know either and Karr was inside with Stefan, so they went to ask Hani. Hani seemed pleased they came to ask him, although his brothers were not pleased, but even then, he did not smile.

"They are Macoran," Catrina said. "Why have they come?"

"They come to barter against their laird's wishes."

"Ah," Catrina muttered.

Perhaps Catrina couldn't think of anything else to say, but Kenna had plenty of questions. "What might be your age?"

"I am second eldest at two and twenty."

"And the others?" Kenna asked as she twirled a lock of her hair.

"Karr is three and twenty. Next after me is Steinn. He is one and twenty.   Magnus is twenty, Nikolas has lived seventeen years, Almoor is fifteen and the wee one is…" Hani scratched the side of his beard.

"Too young to marry?" Kenna asked.

"Aye, though he thinks he is not. Do you fancy him?"

Catrina rolled her eyes. "She fancies every lad she sees, even my brother." She smiled sweetly, grabbed Kenna's hand and pulled her away. "Come, we shall see if there are any onions worthy of pulling in the garden."

Kenna scoffed, "You know there are not, we have not yet planted them." She glanced back at Hani, tipped her head as though she had no choice, and went off with her friend.

*

Muriel was not the only Macoran woman who found the Vikings tempting, but she was the only one with a plan. The arrangement to barter with the MacGreagors was a well-kept secret so far, and since her father was one of the three, and their farm was closest to the MacGreagor village, she had a little bartering of her own to do. First, Muriel had to convince her father to sell one of their cows. The MacGreagors only have four and the Vikings could drink that much milk and eat that much cheese by themselves, she pointed out. It was for the good of both clans, for who knew if the hungry Vikings could easily become thieves?

Her father finally agreed, on one condition – it was up to her to drive the cow to the MacGreagor village, and she could only take the one the whole family hated, for it was the most stubborn cow of them all. She thanked her father, and as soon as he had gone with the other men to the MacGreagor village, she quickly bathed in the river, washed her hair, put on her best clothes, and set off.

Driving the most stubborn cow in the world was not easy. It took nearly half an hour to drive the animal from the river to the path and even then, it turned the wrong way. Putting a rope around her neck hadn't helped because the cow refused to be pulled, so Muriel had no choice, but to pick up a stick and encourage the stubborn cow by smacking it from behind on the rump. That only worked a few steps at a time before the cow spotted another tempting lump of grass and stopped to eat.

Muriel yelled, smacked the cow, and yelled some more. It didn't appear she would get there anytime soon, but she was determined. At last, the cow turned down the path that led to the MacGreagor courtyard. Yet, it was not Muriel or her stick that got the cow moving. It was the buzz of a bee near the cow's ear that did the trick. All of a sudden, the cow kicked its hind legs high in the air, lunged forward, and took off running.

Muriel ran as fast as she could to catch it. "Nay!" she shouted. This was not what she had in mind at all. Caught between knowing she best catch the cow, and wanting to look her best to attract the attention of the Vikings, Muriel tried to flatten her unruly red hair as she ran and it slowed her down.

In the middle of the courtyard, the dogs began to bark, the chickens squawked and sprinted out of the way, the people ran, and Magnus turned around just in time to see the disaster headed his way. Too late, he realized the cow was heading straight for him. He began to wildly flail his arms to force the cow to stop or at least turn away, but the cow would not be persuaded, and his eyes grew even wider.

"Run, brother," Hani shouted. A second later, he watched as the cow lowered its head, burrowed it between Magnus' legs, tossed the Viking out of the way, and kept going. It was Grant who quickly grabbed the cow's rope and managed to halt it.

Magnus landed on his back, whispered something that sounded a lot like, "Ugh," and closed his eyes. The next thing he knew, Muriel was kneeling beside him and had his hand in hers.

"Forgive me...I...are you hurt?"

He was quite certain his eyes would never uncross, but little by little, her face came into focus. Hers was the most bonnie face he had ever seen. She had red hair the color of Kenna's, lips that looked inviting, and eyes that made him feel more alive than he ever had before.

"I only wished to barter the cow," Muriel moaned, as she worriedly patted the back of his hand.

She was about to cry, or Magnus thought, and he should have gotten up to show he was unharmed, but he was far too happy holding her hand. "Fear not, I shall live," he managed to whimper.

"Aye, but *she* shall not," Kenna said behind her. "Muriel Macoran, you ran the cow into him on purpose."

Muriel let go of Magnus' hand, stood up, and turned her glare on Kenna. "I most certainly dinna?"

"Everyone knows you trick lads, hoping to get a husband."

She put her hands on her hips. "Everyone knows what *you alone* tell them."

"I doubt that." Kenna failed to notice all the people gathered in the courtyard watching her, or that most of them were snickering. She turned her ire on Magnus next. "I saw the way you held her hand. Let it not happen again!"

Magnus sat up, hopped to his feet and grabbed Kenna around the waist. "You have chosen me?"

"What?" she gasped.

"Is it not clear?" he asked. When he saw the puzzled look on her face, he let go of her. "You have *not* chosen me?"

She wrinkled her brow. "I might have...I cannae be certain just yet." She leaned around him to look at Grant, but when he did not protest, she sighed and looked up at the man in front of her again. She wondered if it would give her neck a sprain if she had to look up at him too often. That thought made her frown all the more, and without another word, she slowly walked away. Everyone was still laughing, even Catrina, but she was so deep in thought, Kenna didn't notice.

Magnus looked at Hani and shrugged. "Did I do it wrongly?"

Hani ignored him. Instead, he watched the rhythmic sway of Muriel's skirt as she calmly went to fetch the cow Grant was holding. For Grant, her smile was sincere and his matched hers.

Catrina quickly looked to see if Kenna noticed, but Kenna had gone home, even without her mother first calling.

*

Inside the castle, Karr opened the door to see what was happening just in time to see the whole thing. He too smiled, and when he looked at Catrina, his smiling eyes once more managed to meet hers. It was the first time he had seen her smile and it warmed his heart. Of course, her smile was not for him...not yet.

"What is it?" Stefan asked.

"A cow got loose," Karr answered. He closed the door and took a seat at the table next to Stefan across from the farmers. He was more than fascinated to learn how bartering was done in Scotland. As it turned out, it was no different than at home.

"We can sell but two horses without Ronan knowing," Alton said in a low voice as if someone might be able to overhear. "Perhaps, once the colts are weaned..."

"Aye, 'tis better to train them when they are young anyway." Stefan agreed.

Alton opened one of the sacks, dumped out the contents and then emptied the other one out as well. The last one contained the much needed pot for the Vikings to cook in.

"How much for it all?" Stefan asked.

"What can you offer?"

Stefan nodded.

Karr opened the small leather pouch and began to count the gold coins. When he got to three, he stopped to see if he had Stefan's approval. He did, it was enough.

"English money?" Alton asked before he remembered he was talking to a Viking. He smiled, "Of course, 'tis English. We hate the English too, save when we want something from them."

"You barter with them?" Karr asked.

"Only when we have no choice," Stefan answered.

"I suspect the cow is the one my daughter brought to barter," said Alton. "She claims you need another."

Stefan returned Alton's grin. "We can never have too many. How much for the cow?"

Karr opened his purse again, but then handed the whole thing to Stefan. It seemed silly to be handling the money. He watched Stefan count out a few more coins and hand them to Alton. After that, he sat back and listened while Stefan made a bargain for grain and wheat to be delivered after the harvest.

"What news have you of Ronan?" Stefan asked when the bartering was done.

"We cannae believe it, but he won fairly," Alton answered, "and he has some supporters among the young lads. He bribes them with promises of new cottages and the wife of their choice."

Stefan was disgusted. "Even if the lasses are not willing?"

"Aye, but then, it has always been thusly so for the Macorans."

Stefan asked, "What do you mean to do?"

"What can we do?" Alton asked. "Until he does something unthinkable, we cannae kill him. 'Tis not our way. Besides, he is well guarded now."

"Shall you give him Catrina to keep the alliance?" one of the other farmers asked.

"Nay," both Stefan and Karr said.

Stefan half smiled at Karr's response. "We dinna give our daughters to such as he."

Alton nodded. "He means to marry a Brodie if you do not." Exasperated, Alton hung his head. "I cannae think how we let this happen."

"I hoped he might challenge me for Anundi's sword, but he did not," said Stefan. "I would have gladly killed him for you."

"He is simple, but not completely witless." When Alton stood up to go, so did the other men. "He knows he cannae fight you and survive. Nay, there shall be a better way. Perhaps Davie shall challenge him again. We are encouraging it."

"'Tis good to hear. Do send word if he does, we would like to watch."

"I shall." Alton nodded and then led the others out the door. The Macorans glanced around to see if they were being watched and saw no one, but just in case, they hurried to the woods, gathered their horses, and went home.

\*

A few minutes later, Carson shouted from his post on the wall, "Brodies!" Instantly, the people began to scatter. Stefan and Karr ran out of the Castle, just before Catrina and the other women started ushering the children in.

"I say we give them something to see," Karr shouted. All seven Vikings ran to get their shields, helmets, bows, and arrows. In a flash, they were back, scaling the wall and spreading out on top of it. Not long after, Stefan joined them. They spread apart, loaded their bows and got ready to fire.

"Eight of them?" one muttered.

Curious, they stayed to watch until the giant Vikings looked like they were truly taking aim. Instantly, three Brodie warriors scrambled out of the bushes, mounted their horses, and raced away.

\*

All the ground in the garden had finally been overturned and prepared for  planting. Every year, Catrina helped carefully sow the seeds and took great pleasure in watching the plants grow. Of course, some of the seeds would not sprout and when they did not, the planting would be done a second time. The weeds had no trouble at all growing and later, it would be up to other children to pull them before they got too big. The trick was in knowing which plant was a weed and which would produce something to eat. Their labors were heavy, but at least it was never mundane.

Catrina was hard at work in the garden when she spotted Kenna walking toward Grant and stopped to watch.

Kenna just had to know, so she clasped her hands behind her back and slowly strolled up to Grant. "Have you seen Laird Brodie's daughters?"

Always suspicious of Kenna's inquires; Grant asked a question of his own. "Why do you wish to know?"

"Can you not just answer the question? Have you seen them or not?"

"I have not seen them, but a Brodie hunter mentioned they are not yet claimed."

"Because they are unsightly?"

Grant pulled a cloth out of his belt and wiped the sweat off his forehead. "He dinna say, but the eldest is nearly twenty."

"Twenty? 'Tis very old indeed, and to be unmarried still? What else do the Brodie hunters say?"

Grant's mouth curled into a smile. "They warned of a pack of gray wolves last month."

Kenna was instantly annoyed. "Everyone knows that. What else? I mean what do they say of the sisters?"

"Very little. The hunters fear their laird will sell them into slavery if they say anything."

"I see."

She moved a pebble with the toe of her shoe. "I saw how you smiled at Muriel. Have you not been warned? She will use all measure of trickery to get a husband."

"What sort of trickery?"

"Then you have not noticed?" Kenna was certain she had warned him before. "'Tis the sort by which she lets a cow nearly kill a Viking. Do you fancy her?"

"Do you fancy the Vikings?"

Kenna wasn't expecting that question and wasn't sure how to answer. "Some of them...some of the time."

"Then I fancy Muriel some of the time." Grant hid his smile, went back to work and tried to ignore her. He heard Kenna huff her displeasure, looked back, saw her walk away, and then looked to see if Muriel was watching. He couldn't spot her, but that didn't mean Muriel wasn't there.

Kenna stopped and turned around. It wasn't hard to figure out what Grant was looking for. She spotted a pail of water, picked it up, and started back. Just as she got ready to throw the water on Grant, Magnus unwittingly walked between them. The water hit him square in the face and at first, he was shocked, but then his grin widened. "You *do* choose me."

Stunned, Kenna tried to back away. "I…I dinna mean…I mean, I was…oh, no…" He had a look in his eye, as though he was going to grab her and maybe even kiss her. Kenna dropped the pail and tried to get away, but she moved too late.

Magnus leaned down, grabbed her around the legs and slung her over his shoulder.

"Put me down!" she screamed as she pounded both fists on his back. It didn't help.

He carried her to the loch, waded out a couple of feet and dumped her in. "I dinna mean to get you wet either." Just as quickly, he turned, walked out of the water, and went back to work.

All the MacGreagors were laughing at her and Kenna was furious. She loudly shrieked her frustration and beat the water with her hands, which made them laugh even harder. At last, Hani took pity on her, waded in, reached out his hand, and pull her up. "Thank you," she managed to say. Her clothes embarrassingly clung to her body, there was mud on her bottom and she simply couldn't get home fast enough. Even after she stepped inside and closed the door, she could still hear them laughing. It would be weeks before they stopped teasing her about it, and she doubted she could bear it.

*

Nothing could have surprised the MacGreagors more the next day, than to see three Macoran warriors ride into the village. It was not who they were that surprised them, but what they wanted.

As usual, Stefan was working in the garden. He walked down the hill to the courtyard where other MacGreagors had already gathered, just as Kenna and Catrina came out of the Keep to see what was happening.

"Laird Macoran invites the MacGreagor unmarrieds to a feast."

"For what reason?" Stefan asked.

"He means to choose a bride. He invites all the unmarried of the MacGreagors, the Limonds, and the Brodies."

"You mean he wishes to choose *Catrina* as his bride," William said. He was not surprised when the warrior nodded.

"When?" Stefan wanted to know.

"In two days," the warrior answered.

Stefan nodded. "Tell him I shall consider it."

"We go now to invite the Brodies. May I tell them they may cross your land?"

"Aye, we shall not stop them if they come in peace. See that they dinna capture you."

The Macoran spokesman oddly smiled. "They shall not capture us." He nodded, turned his horse, rode between the loch and the wall, and then led his men down the path toward the Brodie village.

Stefan rubbed his brow. "What do you suppose Ronan is truly up to?"

William shrugged, "A feast with the Brodies? He has gone daft. I say we stay home. I'll not have him choosing Kenna either."

"I say you are right. We shall let the Brodies cross our land, and let them think we dinna care if Ronan marries one of Laird Brodie's daughters."

William paused before he said, "'Tis the best choice for us all." He walked back up the hill with Stefan and continued to talk of other things.

As soon as she could no longer hear them, Catrina shrugged and started to go back inside, but not before she looked to see if Karr was watching her. He was, and she should not have looked. Next time, she would not look, even if it killed her.

Kenna quickly followed her friend into the castle. "Do you suppose Laird Brodie's son will come?"

"Ah, you fancy him again, I see."

"Perhaps."

"And perhaps not?" Catrina asked.

"I simply cannae decide which is the most handsome."

"Kenna, there is more to a lad than how handsome he is. He must be honest, good, and kind."

"Like Karr?"

"Why do you say, like Karr?"

Kenna brushed the side of Catrina's long hair back over her friend's shoulder. "Everyone has seen the way you look at each other. Even his brothers speak of it. I think he fancies you and I think you fancy him as well. Did I not wager you would marry within the year?"

"In twenty or thirty years, perhaps."

Kenna laughed. "You suppose he shall wait that long for you? I wager he shall give up, and marry another if you do not claim him soon."

"Claim him? Lasses dinna claim lads."

"They do if they are wise, and in this clan, there is no other way."

"I see, then why have you not claimed Grant?"

Kenna sat down at the table, folded her arms and yawned. "You are right. They must claim us before we claim them. Only dinna wait too long, dear friend, for when we go to the feast, Karr shall have many a lass to choose from."

"Dinna you hear our fathers? We are not going to the feast."

Kenna grinned and headed for the door. "I say we shall go. And why not? They let us go to the feasts in autumn." She went out the door and left Catrina alone with her thoughts for a change.

Her family would want bread. They always wanted bread, so Catrina started to gather the ingredients to make it for their evening meal. Nevertheless, being busy didn't keep her from pondering the situation. Was it true? Did everyone suspect she favored Karr? If they did, it was her own fault for looking at him too often. Kenna was right, there were bound to be lasses in other clans with an eye for Karr, but there was little she could do about that. He was old enough to choose and she reminded herself she didn't want to marry this soon anyway.

She stopped her work, stood completely still, and tried to imagine another woman in his arms. She could not stand the idea, and the thought shattered any illusions she might have had about not truly wanting him. She did want to be in his arms...she wanted it desperately. Yet, there were too many mouths to feed to consider marriage. Then again, they were not her children. On the other hand, what would they do without her?

Catrina shrugged and concentrated on making enough flat breads to once more fill their empty stomachs. Taking a husband was a lot more complicated than she thought.

*

A look here and there was not enough and Karr needed to find a reason to talk to Catrina alone. It had not been easy with his brothers always around, but on this morning, Magnus and Steinn decided to go hunting. Obbi went with them, just to see if he could find that rabbit again. Hani liked the accomplishment he felt as the wall steadily increased in length, and was happily helping the other men. Almoor kept busy entertaining the little ones, for which the mothers were eternally grateful, and Nikolas was busy cooking. Therefore, Karr finally had Catrina all to himself.

Because there were never enough lower tree branches upon which to spread wet clothing, the MacGreagor women washed on different days. Even then, a curious animal would sometimes try to make off with an article or two, so the clothes had to be checked on often. With so many in her family, Catrina's washing took nearly the whole day. Her labors were lessoned when Kenna had time to help, but on this day, Kenna's mother had given her other duties to do. Catrina's sister normally helped too, but Stefan had her planting seeds in the garden instead. In fact, everyone was busy with other chores.

At least, it was a bright sunny day and getting soaking wet, as she always did, didn't mean getting bone chilling cold as well. She carried her full basket out of the Keep, went to the edge of the loch, and dumped the clothes in the water. She set the basket on a rock, waded in, and began to wash each article. She rubbed them with soap, diligently tried to get the stains out, and then rinsed each. Wringing the water out of the heavy wool hurt her wrists, but it had to be done.

It was not until she had her basket nearly full of wet clothes that she discovered Karr standing on the shore watching her. He was the last person she wanted to see. She looked a fright, she was tired and her hands hurt. "Have you nothing to do?"

"You are being watched."

"By you, at least." She decided to ignore him and went back to wringing out Conan's long pants.

"By a lass in the bushes," Karr said, pointing toward the path that led to the Macoran land.

Catrina stopped long enough to look that direction. "'Tis only Muriel. She would do better to come help me instead of just watching."

"Should I tell her?"

At first, Catrina thought to turn him down, but why not? She could use the help and Muriel could come out of hiding for a change. "If you wish."

"Nay, if *you* wish."

"I do wish it."

"Or...I could help you," he hesitantly said.

"A lad doing the washing?"

"In our land, if a lad asks a lass to do his washing, they are the same as promised. Therefore, my brothers and I are accustomed to doing it ourselves."

She wrung out Conan's tunic, tossed it in the basket and looked for more in the water. Thankfully, that was the last of it. The basket was already heavier than she could carry, so she usually just dragged it to the trees instead. Catrina waded out of the water, wrung out the bottom of her shirt, and when she reached for the basket, Karr picked it up.

She stared into his eyes briefly, quickly looked away and headed for the nearest tree. "Your clan dinna think less of you for it?"

"If they did, they dinna say."

"I can see why. Are all Vikings as big as you?" She took the first article of clothing out of the basket and spread it on the lower branch of a Black Alder tree.

"A few."

"Are the lasses tall as well?"

"About your same height, perhaps a little taller."

"You dinna wish to marry any of them?"

"'Twas not what Grandfather wished. Had we married, we should not have seen Scotland."

"But you did fancy one or two, am I right?"

"Aye, one or two." He found her questions a bit puzzling, but at least she was talking to him. "What do they do at a feast in Scotland?"

Catrina smiled at the thought of a happier subject. "They are wondrous. There are games for the children, when the children are invited. The Macoran's cook fresh river salmon and there is always more than enough to eat."

"What else?"

Catrina reached into the basket for another article of clothing and moved to a higher branch. "Normally, the feasts are held after the harvest. In spring, there will likely be less. Yet, dried fruit, if there be any left, shall be moistened and baked in pies." She paused to think about it. "'Tis quite early in spring for a feast."

"Your father does not wish us to go?"

"He does not wish *me* to go, but I see no reason why others cannae. Perhaps you might persuade him."

"How?"

"Well, you might mention 'tis one meal we shall not have to give to seven hungry brothers."

Karr grinned. "You are wise as well as..." He remembered what she said and caught himself before he flattered her. Instead, he set the basket down, pulled a tunic out, wrung it out a second time, and spread it higher in the tree than she could reach.

Catrina put her hands on her hips. "And how am I to get it down?"

"You shall need my help then, too."

"I…" Just then, she was distracted. The children were laughing and as she watched, Obbi came around the corner of the castle on stilts. The little ones were thrilled, and even she was delighted…that is, until it looked like he was going to fall. Her smile quickly faded.

"Dinna fret, he has been walking on stilts since he was but five."

"He pretends he shall fall?" she asked.

"Aye."

"The lads walk on stilts to pick the fruit of the trees. 'Twill be a very fine chore for him come Autumn."

Karr reached in the basket just as she did and touched her hand. She quickly withdrew it, so he pulled the next article of clothing out, rung it out, handed it to her, and followed as she went to the other side of the tree. "Do you fear me?" he couldn't help but ask.

"Nay, should I?"

"You should not. I…we gave your father our pledge that we would not hurt any lass, and we shall keep it."

"Then I do not fear you."

"But you fear Ronan?"

She sighed. "I do not fear him; I fear a war with the Brodies if he forms an alliance."

"But you do wish to marry, am I right?"

She looked him in the eye for a change. "I dinna wish to have more children to care for. Besides, who would care for all my father's children if I marry?"

"Perhaps your father could marry again."

She looked for her father in the garden where he usually was and found him. He and a few other men were hard at work and not paying any attention to anything else. Grant was watching her, however. "'Tis doubtful. Father shows no interest in any of the unmarried lasses."

"Perhaps we might help him."

Catrina started to smile. "Plot against him, you mean?"

"Aye, a lad needs a wife and your father more than most."

She took another pair of long pants out of the basket and handed it to Karr to wring out. He was able to get a lot more water out of them, which meant they would dry faster. She found it odd Grant was watching her and glanced at him a second time. Maybe she was wrong. Maybe Grant did prefer her instead of Kenna or Muriel. Nevertheless, she was long since past preferring him. "Perhaps we might find Father a wife at the feast?"

"Perhaps," said Karr, "but only if you are there to help. I'd not know the right kind of lass for him."

Catrina glanced at Stefan again. "Father shall never let me go."

"He will if you ask him. I see the love he has for you in his eyes, more so than for any of his other children."

"I remind him of Mother, or so he says." She found another branch and truly considered the idea. "Nay, Ronan shall surely choose me and then Father shall have to fight him. I cannae let that happen...nay, 'tis too foolhardy."

"If Ronan chooses you, I shall challenge him before your father can."

Catrina giggled. "His head is probably still hurting from the last time he was stupid enough to challenge you."

"Then you agree?"

"I agree, but I doubt Father shall. He has said we are not to go, and rare are the times he changes his mind. Still, I would like Father to be happy the way he was when Mother yet lived." She reached for another item, only to discover the basket was empty. "I thank you for helping me." She picked up the basket and headed home.

"Dinna look back," she said under her breath as she glanced around, "dinna look back for now they are all watching us."

# CHAPTER 10

She tried, but when Catrina asked if they could attend the feast, her father was unmovable. When she could, she passed the word to Karr, who promised he would give it a try. It was late at night when Karr and Stefan sat down at the table in the Keep to talk. The village was quiet, the children were in bed, and even the dogs were taking a nap.

"'You fancy Catrina?" Stefan asked.

"Aye, she is wise and works very hard...too hard."

Stefan bowed his head. "All our lasses work too hard. Until the clan grows, there is little time for leisure."

"Then why not let them go to the feast?"

"I would if all were invited. Ronan asks that I bring only the unmarried. He is up to something, but I cannae guess precisely what. If all he wanted was my daughter, I would challenge him and be done with it. Now I fear he wants our land and has made a bargain with the Brodies. 'Tis best if we stay here."

"Laird Limond seems to be a fair-minded lad. Would he not help if the Brodies attack?"

"Aye, we have pledged to help each other."

"Suppose Ronan means to turn the Limonds against the MacGreagors?"

Stefan thought about that. "I cannae see how he could. We have been good friends with the Limonds for years."

"Will the Limonds find it an insult if we dinna go to the feast?"

Stefan stood up, walked to a table against the wall, and brought back two goblets and a flask of wine. "I had not thought of that."

"In our country, not accepting an invitation is an insult. Perhaps even the Brodies might be insulted."

"Aye, but Ronan is not nearly clever enough to think of that?"

"He has wise counsel, perhaps."

"Who? Who would be witless enough to help Ronan?"

"I know not, but I say we go to the feast and find out."

Stefan poured wine into both goblets and took a long drink. "Does my daughter wish to go?"

"All lasses wish for a day of fun instead of work."

"True." Stefan took another swallow and frowned. "Does she complain?"

"She loves you and the children too much to complain."

"Do you promise to help me watch over Catrina if I take her?"

"I am more than willing to fight Ronan."

Stefan grinned. "If you can catch him."

Karr returned his smile. "Then 'tis settled. We go to the feast?"

"It means leaving the clan unprotected."

"True, but how shall the Brodies know?"

"They know far more than we suspect. I have seen Laird Brodie's son hiding atop the hill watching us."

"You send no spies of your own to watch them?"

"Nay, I cannae let a lad be captured and sold. 'Tis dangerous enough just to send out the hunters. All we truly need to know is when the Brodies are about to attack."

"I agree," said Karr. He downed the rest of his drink and set the goblet down.

"The feast could be a trap."

"How so?"

Stefan paused to contemplate what he was about to say. "The feast is for all the unmarried. 'Tis possible they mean to draw our strongest lads away from the village."

"'Tis possible, but if our lads sound the alarm, we shall not be very far away?"

Stefan finally stood up. "We have lived in fear of the Brodies too long. 'Tis time to face the old goat and have it out. Perhaps he shall do me the pleasure of letting me kill him finally."

Karr stood up, nodded, and went to the door. "My brothers and I thank you."

"And Catrina?"

"Aye, but my brothers want wives and they shall be most grateful. They talk of nothing else, and at the feast, there should be plenty of lasses to choose from."

"Does Magnus not have his heart set on Kenna?"

"Nay, but he likes jesting with her very much." Karr smiled and walked out the door.

On the second floor landing, Catrina heard the door close and hurried to get into bed before her father came up the stairs. Karr had done it…he had talked her father into letting them go to the feast, and she was deliriously happy. If she thought she could without her father hearing her, she would slip out and tell Kenna, but she had to wait. That night, she was so excited it took an unusually long time to fall asleep. She thought of putting flowers in her hair, of making certain her clothes were as clean as possible, and perhaps one of the women would let her borrow a linen undergarment. Perhaps Muriel's mother might, but then, Muriel was probably going.

Before she could make definite plans, Catrina fell asleep.

*

Of the unmarried in the MacGreagor clan, Stefan asked Karr, Hani, Magnus, Grant, Donahue, Garth, Catrina, and Kenna, to accompany him to the Macoran feast. Steinn elected to stay home and help with whatever still needed to be done. They had just gathered their horses and were about to mount them when Wallace whistled, and every head turned toward the wall.

"Brodies," Wallace announced.

Still afraid it was a trap, Stefan asked, "How many?"

Wallace held up his hand while he counted and then turned to answer, "Ten lads and five lasses. Father, Laird Brodie is not with them."

Worried, the lines in Stefan's forehead deepened. "He stays to attack us."

"Nay, Father, he sends his son. He shall not attack so long as his son is with us."

"Wallace is right," Karr said.

"Aye, he is," Stefan agreed. "We wait. 'Tis better to be behind than in front of them." He was impressed when he saw the Viking brothers move to stand in front of Kenna and Catrina, but he didn't have much time to consider it before he heard the pounding of horse's hooves on the hard earth.

In the lead, Branan Brodie slowed as he rounded the end of the wall, and just as Wallace said, he brought only ten men and five women into the MacGreagor village. Branan halted his horse a few feet away from the MacGreagor laird, dismounted and nodded to show his respect. "'Tis good of you to allow us safe passage."

His friendly manner caught Stefan off guard. He fully expected the son to be just like the father. "We care not to fight with the Brodies. Where might your father be?"

Branan had a glint of mischief in his eye when he answered. "He fully intended to come, for he too is without a wife, but a sudden illness has befallen him."

Stefan almost smiled. "Are others unwell?"

"Nay, 'tis one of a kind. There is nothing Father likes better than crabapple juice sweetened with honey and cinnamon." Kenna, Branan noticed, was being well guarded and he could barely see her peeking between two of the Vikings. His eyes met hers finally, but he didn't smile at her.

"Aye, but the crabapples are far from ripe this time of year," said Stefan.

Branan tried not to smile, but he couldn't help himself. "I suspect that might be the cause." He remembered his manners and reached his hand out toward the two women still on horses behind him. "My sisters; Aerica and Liliam."

Stefan nodded to each of them. "Might they be twins?"

"They are, and they are much favored in our clan."

"I can see why, they are quite the bonnie lasses." Stefan found their bashfulness enchanting.

"You shall understand then, that I shall not let them marry just any lad."

Stefan was pretty sure he knew what Branan was hinting at. "I feel the same about my daughters."

"Then we agree?"

Stefan completely agreed, but he did not show how pleased he was. "We do. If you care to lead the way, the MacGreagors shall follow you."

"Why not ride with me, Laird MacGreagor? There is much to discuss."

"Very well." Stefan waited until the others were mounted and then got on his horse. He made certain Catrina and Kenna were well protected and then joined Branan Brodie at the head of the procession. At last, he smiled. "I have seen odder days than this, but not many."

Branan returned his smile. "Riding beside a Brodie, you mean?"

"Aye."

"I hear," Branan said as they walked their horses down the path, and then turned toward the Macoran village, "Ronan Macoran wishes to choose a wife this day."

"Aye, he means to choose my daughter."

"So I have heard. It is true the MacGreagors allow a lass to choose instead?"

"Aye. I ask you this? How many Brodie lads and lasses are happy in their marriage?"

Branan took a moment to think about that. "Not many, I fear. Certainly my mother was not happy, nor was my father, though he would never admit it."

"A lad who chooses wrongly does not often admit his mistake."

"Nay, he does not, but a lass can choose wrongly as well."

"Perhaps, but if he choose her, and she can say nay, then the unhappiness may be avoided. If she says aye, then she finds him suitable and they have a chance at happiness."

"I see your meaning."

When Stefan saw Alton Macoran's mouth drop, and then start to walk toward them, he raised his hand and halted the procession. He smiled to reassure his friend and then waited until he was close enough to be heard.

"My eyes deceive me," Alton said. "Are these not Brodies?"

"Aye," Stefan answered. "They are the friendly sort of Brodies."

Alton looked a little dumbstruck. "My Muriel begs to go, but I have not the time to take her. May she ride with you?"

"Aye," Stefan answered.

"Will you see Ronan does not marry her?" Alton asked.

Stefan chuckled. "She shall be safe with us."

Alton turned, waved to his daughter, and wasn't surprised when she quickly mounted a horse and headed that way. "Does she not seem a bit too eager?"

Again, Stefan chuckled, "'Tis a feast, after all."

"That must be it." Alton nodded to his daughter as she fell in line beside Grant, and then watched as the procession continued to move on. When they were gone, he looked long and hard toward the MacGreagor village. "Has Laird Brodie passed?" he wondered aloud.

*

On a path just wide enough for two, Kenna and Catrina rode behind several Brodies, Karr and Hani, and in front of Magnus and Garth. When they started moving again, Kenna slumped. "Splendid, Muriel is with us. I suppose I shall have to be kind to her."

"Indeed you shall," Catrina agreed. "Father asks that we be kind to everyone this day."

"Well, he is our laird, so I shall try...no matter how it gripes my very soul."

"Your soul shall survive. I intend to have all the pleasures afforded us. After all, we've not had a day of rest in…weeks."

Kenna glanced up at the clear blue sky. "True, we deserve a day of pleasures and it dinna look like rain for once."

"Then you shall leave Muriel be and not plague her?"

"I dinna plague Muriel." Offended, Kenna put her nose in the air and looked away. She ignored Catrina's giggle and looked behind her just to see where Muriel was. She was riding beside Grant, of all things, and Garth seemed happy to see her too. Kenna rolled her eyes and turned back to face front.

*

"Would you be opposed to a Brodie choosing a MacGreagor to marry?" Branan was asking.

Stefan cast his eyes downward. "Do you mean simply to forge an alliance?"

"Nay, I mean if a Brodie desires to make a MacGreagor lass happy, shall he be allowed to ask?"

"We have hated the Brodies for years. 'Tis not likely we shall give our daughters to a clan that sells lads into slavery."

"And if the Brodies give up that practice?"

Stefan looked into the sincere eyes of the man who would likely be the next Brodie laird. "Is there not a fortune yet to be had?"

"Perhaps, but 'tis not easy being hated. We are hated by more than just the Limonds, the Macorans, and the MacGreagors. There are clans on all sides of us with whom we do not find favor."

"Because you capture them?"

"Because my father and his father captured them."

"You shall not?"

"MacGreagor, we have jewels and pleasures in our storehouses three generations cannae use up. What we need, is to come and go without fear."

"You fear us?"

Branan glanced back at the Vikings. "Them, I do." He smiled at Stefan and continued. "This be the first feast I have yet to see. We hear of them, we long for them, but we are never asked to come. Our lads must marry Brodies, like it or not, for no other clan will let us have their daughters."

Stefan had never looked at it like that before. "Still, 'tis hard to change the minds of the people. Most have grown up hating the Brodies."

"I know, and I hardly blame them. Of course, I can do little until my father and his council are no longer with us."

"You could fight him."

"Aye, but 'twould cause a wound in the hearts of my sisters that would not heal. He is a lad without mercy, but not to them. To them, he is a good and kind father whom they dearly love. I love him too, when he is not…without mercy."

Stefan held his breath as he asked the next question, "Tell me, have you a particular MacGreagor lass in mind?"

"Aye, she has the red hair of the Macoran."

"Kenna? I see." When it wasn't Catrina, Stefan allowed himself to exhale. "Her parents were Macoran before they became MacGreagors."

"Her father will not agree, I take it."

"'Tis doubtful."

"I thought as much."

*

"I cannae hear them. Of what do Laird Brodie's son and your father speak?" Kenna asked, nodding to the third farmer with his mouth agape as they passed.

"They speak of you, I am quite certain. 'Tis a pity your father made Donahue vow not to let a lad could carry you off," Catrina teased.

She looked behind her again. I believe Donahue has forgotten. He is talking to a Brodie, if you can imagine. Never did I think we should abide them, let alone ride with them."

"They dinna look so very frightening up close. They look like..."

"Us?"

Catrina nodded. "Aye, like us. I say we become friends for this day at least."

"I agree. I tire of always being frightened. What do you suppose Donahue and the Brodie are talking about?"

"The Vikings," Catrina answered. "The Brodie no doubt has a thousand questions, at least. As do I."

"What sort of questions?" Kenna asked.

"I do not care to say where they may hear me."

"You? Shy suddenly?" Kenna asked. "Go on, ask them." She flexed the muscles in her left bicep the way she had seen Grant do a time or two. "I shall protect you."

Catrina giggled. "Very well, I wish to know about the land of their birth. Father says 'tis just as green as Scotland?"

"It is," Karr answered, "though there are far more mountains and the mountains are much closer to the sea."

Catrina giggled. "There, you see, Karr hears everything we say."

"He has ears to hear, indeed," Kenna agreed. "What do you suppose will happen...I mean with Laird Macoran...when he asks for you again."

"I dinna know, but Father still says he shall never allow it. I say we eat our fill, and pay no mind to Laird Macoran. It is said, Ronan cannae hear anyway."

"Who besides Muriel says that?"

"Who have we seen but Muriel?" Catrina asked.

"True, but can we believe her?" She suddenly had an idea. "I wonder that she does not want to be mistress of the Macorans. Come to think of it, 'twould be a perfect match. She is as simple as Ronan."

"Kenna, you are being unkind."

"Truthful is not unkind."

"Well, I like Muriel. She is...resourceful."

"Aye, when she wants to marry a Viking."

"Does she? Has she said as much?" Catrina asked.

"Well no, but you do not think that cow came to us accidentally."

"I thought she brought the cow at her father's wish. Did we not barter for it, Karr?"

"Aye, we did." Karr answered.

"There, you see. She was not trying to trick one of the brothers after all. Besides, I thought you said she favors Grant, or is it that Grant favors her?"

Kenna turned to look behind her again. "Just now I am reminded." She looked beyond each set of riders until she laid eyes on Grant. "He rides with Muriel still."

"Does he?" Catrina turned to look too, and smiled when she spotted them. They seemed to delight in each other's good company. "I think 'tis a good match."

"A good match? Are you daft?"

"Aye," Catrina said.

In front of her, Karr smiled. Hani did not smile, but then, he never did.

*

It took two full days, but when he awoke on the morning of the feast, the new Macoran Laird miraculously had his hearing back. However, no one else knew that. He sat at the table in his Keep and listened as his advisors and protectors talked about him. Occasionally, one would come close and yell something. To that, he nodded or shook his head appropriately, and then asked a question totally unrelated. He was being magnificently cunning and sly, at least he thought so, but when the door opened, Ronan couldn't help but look up. He quickly recovered himself and looked down at the table again.

Davie suspected it and intentionally turned away so Ronan could not read his lips. "The Brodies are coming," he said to the other men, "and the MacGreagors come with them."

Ronan forgot himself and abruptly stood up. "They ride together?"

Shocked, the other men turned to stare at him. "You can hear after all?" Davie sneered. "Our laird is a deceiver and a cheat."

"I just now recovered," Ronan lied. "How far away are the Brodies?"

"But a few minutes," the man at the door answered.

"Does Catrina come with the MacGreagors?" Ronan asked.

"Aye."

Ronan slowly grinned, but his delight quickly faded. "The Brodies and the MacGreagors ride together, though? What does it mean?"

Davie reached for the door latch, "It means this shall be a good day for all the Macorans, save perhaps you." He yanked the door open and went to stand in the courtyard to welcome their guests. He could see the Limonds standing on their barges, and the Macoran men pulled them across the river. He decided he best warn Laird Limond, so he quickly walked to the river, extended his hand to Mistress Limond and helped her ashore. Then he did the same for her husband.

"You shall be greatly pleased when you hear the news, I think," Davie said.

"What?" Laird Limond asked. "Have you done away with Ronan?"

Davie smiled. "Not yet, but he was convinced to make me his second in command."

"That is a relief. At least some of the Macorans have their heads on straight."

"Ronan's hearing has returned, but that is not the best news. The Brodies shall be here soon – and the MacGreagors ride with them."

Laird Limond's jaw dropped. "Indeed? With them and not behind them?"

"With them and word is, some are joyful and even laughing."

"Laughing? I dinna know the old goat knew how to laugh."

"'Tis not the old goat, 'tis his son."

Laird Limond was more than a little dubious. "Will wonders never cease. First we gladly welcome Vikings into our midst and now Brodies? This, I must see for myself."

*

Word that the Brodies were coming spread quickly among the Macoran and Limond clans. Most of them had not seen the Brodies either, but they knew the MacGreagors, so it wasn't hard to spot them. The young Macoran boys were ready, and as soon as Stefan and Branan dismounted, they led the first of the horses away.

"'Tis true, I see." Laird Limond said, coming to greet them. "Never did I think I should see this day."

"Nor did we," Branan admitted. As soon as his sisters dismounted and their horses were led away, he introduced them to Laird Limond. "Tell me; was it your idea to invite us?"

"Nay," Laird Limond said, "I wish I had thought of it, save for..."

Branan smiled, "Save for fear of the old goat would come?"

Laird Limond was completely taken aback. "You know we call him that."

Branan leaned a little closer, "We called him that long before any of you."

Laird Limond put a hand on Stefan's shoulder. "I like him, MacGreagor."

"As do I," Stefan said.

*

Catrina and Kenna had to wait their turn to dismount, but as soon as they did, Catrina slipped up beside Laird Limond's wife. "Father is in want of a lass to care for his many children."

"He wants a wife?" she asked.

"Perhaps he does not want just yet, but he needs one."

"Does he now?" she asked, her grin as wide as Catrina's. "I know just the lass."

"I thought you might." Catrina hugged her and then went back to join Kenna. She kept an eye on Mistress Limond and when she whispered in her husband's ear,

Catrina was certain the rumor would soon spread. As always, Karr was watching her, so she gave him a knowing smile and nodded her success. He looked as pleased as she did.

The feast was truly a sight to behold, for there were tables heavy laden with all manner of foods. Salmon steaks were the main attraction with little boys fanning the flies away. More salmon and chicken were cooking on several square, mud brick fireplaces built just for the occasion. An autumn feast always offered many more delights, but as it was, the Macorans managed to make large pots of stew that included the meat of a wild hog, onions, leeks and cabbage. As well, dried apples, pears and cherries were softened, sweetened with honey, covered with bread dough and baked on griddles over various small fires. Naturally, there were plenty of oat and wheat breads, bowls, goblets, and spoons, plus an abundance of ale and wine flasks to quench a hearty thirst.

"Why do the lasses wear scarves over their heads?" Catrina wondered as they began to stroll through the crowd.

Without Catrina and Kenna realizing it, Muriel was right behind them. "Ronan commanded they do it to show they are married."

Kenna nearly said something spiteful, but when Catrina grabbed her arm, she changed her mind. "Can they not just say they are married?"

"Apparently Ronan thinks they cannot," Muriel answered.

"Where is *His Majesty*?" Kenna asked.

Catrina pointed toward her grandfather's Keep. "There, on the walkway where he might look down on us."

Sure enough, Ronan stood in front of the door with his arms folded staring at Catrina. "He desires you still, I see," said Kenna. When she looked behind her, Grant and Muriel were walking away. She rolled her eyes, "'Tis disgusting," she muttered.

Catrina was about to ask what Kenna was referring to, when a little girl holding a chunk of bread whizzed past. She was being chased by a little boy and it didn't look like the girl would win. It made Catrina smile.

"Just look at them," Kenna groaned.

"Who?"

"Can you not see how all the lasses watch *our* Vikings?"

She glanced around, and her friend was right. Several of the women were gawking at the Vikings. The three of them stood talking to Laird Limond, and while Hani and Magnus seemed to notice, Karr was paying them no mind. "Kenna, as I have said many times, you cannae have them all. Sooner or later, you must choose."

"I know, I know."

Catrina giggled. She knew the Macorans better than the Limonds, but found several to greet in both clans. It was not until later that she realized the Brodies were staying together at the edge of the gathering looking lost and confused. "They know not what to do?" Catrina whispered to Kenna, as she nodded toward the Brodies. "Do you vow to be kind to the twins?"

"Of course I do. I have no vendetta against them. Perhaps they might marry a Viking or two, and then *we* shall have an alliance with the Brodies instead of Ronan."

She ignored the fact that Kenna had just tried to keep all the Vikings for herself. "I fancy that idea." She grabbed Kenna's hand and began to weave her way through the crowd back to the Brodies. As soon as they arrived, she respectfully nodded to Laird Brodie's daughters. "I am Catrina, Laird MacGreagor's daughter."

Kenna had forgotten Branan Brodie's dazzling looks until she stood face to face with him. Suddenly, she was so enamored; she hardly felt it when Catrina tugged on her arm to remind her to greet the twins. "I am Kenna," she barely managed to get out before finally tearing her eyes off Branan's.

"Laird MacGreagor is very handsome," said Aerica while Liliam emphatically nodded.

"Is he?" Catrina asked, "You are very kind to say so. He is unmarried these three years and hopes to find a wife soon."

Kenna's mouth dropped. "'Tis the first I heard of this, Catrina MacGreagor. Does he know he hopes to marry again soon?"

Catrina winked at Liliam. "Not precisely, but I did tell him he needs a wife."

"'Tis what I thought." She took a step closer to the twins. "I am Kenna, and we have heard you were unsightly. We have heard wrong." She made both Aerica and Liliam blush.

"You dinna hate us, Kenna MacGreagor?" Aerica asked.

"Not today. Today we feast."

"Thank you," said Aerica while Liliam emphatically nodded. Aerica turned her attention back to Catrina. "There are many widows among the Brodie clan. Perhaps your father might come to see them someday…after Father dies."

"Is he very ill?" Catrina asked.

"Possibly not, but all fathers die someday," said Liliam.

Thinking of their own fathers, both Catrina and Kenna bowed their heads. "Let us not talk of that," said Catrina.

"May we ask…" Aerica started.

"Indeed. What?" Catrina answered.

"Is Ronan the silly one who stands upon the steps grinning at you?"

Catrina puffed her cheeks. "Aye, and you are right, he is silly."

"We thought so," Liliam said. She nodded toward the brothers. "Are they the Vikings? The hunters say they have seen them, but these are not as big as the story our hunters tell."

Catrina giggled and glanced at the brothers. They were surrounded by the curious and as soon as she spotted him watching her, Karr looked away. "They were standing on the wall."

"I thought so," Liliam confided. She glanced at her brother just to make certain she had not said too much, but Branan only had eyes for Kenna.

"You are so different than we imagined," Kenna admitted. "Are you not hungry? The food is there for the taking and we shall go with you, if you like."

"May we talk to the Vikings first?" Aerica asked.

"Of course you may," Catrina answered.

"Do they hate us too?" Liliam asked.

"Nay," Kenna answered. "They have only just come from across the sea."

Liliam smiled and then nodded. "Then we shall not fear them." She looked to her brother for his nod of approval, took her sister's hand and followed Catrina.

Kenna was about to follow when she put her hands on her hips instead and glared at Branan Brodie. "Are you not coming?"

He was astonished that she would talk to him so bluntly. "I…"

"We cannae learn not to hate the Brodies, if they will not talk to us." She turned her attention to the rest of the Brodies. "If you dinna eat, those that prepared it shall be insulted. Laird MacGreagor and Laird Limond shall not let harm come to anyone this day. Besides, it has been years since the Brodies tried to capture any of us."

Branan nodded to his people, then to her and began to walk beside her.

"The truth be told," she confided, "the MacGreagors need more lasses. The Viking brothers are in want of wives, we have three unmarried lads in the MacGreagor clan, none of which are brave enough to ask of either Catrina or I. I cannae abide a willowy lad. And now, Laird MacGreagor wants a wife, although he already has more children than he..."

"Kenna," Branan said.

"What?"

He glanced back at the members of his clan, noticed they were beginning to mingle and then looked at his smiling sisters. "Laird MacGreagor said that in your clan, the lass must choose the lad."

Kenna giggled. "He means, the lad chooses the lass, and then she says yea or nay. I should die if I were put upon to ask a lad to marry me. 'Twould be unseemly."

"I see." He would have asked her right then, for there was a sparkle in her eye when she looked at him. Yet, bringing a MacGreagor wife home to his father would be complicated at best. He already knew her father would not approve. It was an impossible situation, but he was determined to find a way now more than ever.

While Catrina introduced the twins to each of the Vikings, Kenna did the same for Branan. The twins also had a thousand questions, which Catrina found a bit boring, so she drifted away and went to talk to Muriel and Grant. It wasn't long before Kenna and Branan joined them. Soon, they were filling their bowls with delights and enjoying each other's company.

Karr didn't like the way Ronan was watching Catrina, so he drifted away from his brothers as well. He got something to eat, and stood just a couple of feet behind Catrina. When Ronan spotted him, his eyes widened and he quickly looked away.

# CHAPTER 11

Tired of feeling his beady eyes on her, Catrina turned to face the Keep and nodded toward Ronan. "How has he managed to get the Macorans to obey him?"

"Davie asked that they agree to tolerate him until after the feast," Muriel answered.

Kenna turned to face him as well. "Poor lad, he is not happy."

With three young women and three not so pleased men staring at him, Ronan looked a little flustered, glanced around and finally found a chair to sit on. When he looked back, they were still watching him. He considered others to watch, anyone at all, but his eyes kept coming back to the people with Catrina.

Muriel sighed. "How I miss Laird Macoran. He was a jolly lad always surrounded by friends. The lairds of other clans went to greet him right away, but they ignore Ronan."

"Should I have gone to greet him?" Branan asked.

"Nay," Grant blurted out. "You least of all. He shall see that as your agreement to make an alliance."

"Or worse," Catrina added, "an offer of one of your sisters."

"It seems I have much to learn," Branan admitted.

"Tis quite sad, truly," Muriel said.

"What is?" Branan asked.

Muriel answered, "He supposes all lads would want their daughters married to a laird, and not one Macoran has made him an offer."

"Not even your father?" Kenna snidely asked.

Muriel narrowed her eyes. "I knew you cannae be good for long, Kenna MacGreagor."

"I meant no harm," Kenna argued, but her sarcasm was unmistakable.

"No more than usual," Muriel shot back.

Catrina looked from Muriel to Kenna and then at Branan. Interestingly, Branan was enjoying the banter between them. He liked Kenna, that much she could see, but she wondered if he still would, once he understood what she and Muriel were truly at war over.

"This morning," Muriel said, hoping to change the subject, "Ronan tricked some of the lads into thinking he

could not hear still, when he heard every word. Macorans
are not fond of that kind of trickery."

"Is that why the Macorans avoid him as well?" Catrina
asked. She watched as Ronan's eyes scanned the crowd of
laughing and fun loving people. He seemed particularly
displeased with the way the other clans were accepting the
Brodies.

Branan wrinkled his brow. "Who might that be?" he
asked, nodding toward the man climbing up the steps to say
something to Ronan. Ronan nodded and the man went back
down the steps.

"Davie," Muriel answered. "'Tis Davie we want to lead
us, but he lost the race."

As Muriel explained what happened, Catrina once more
wandered away. Karr was not far behind her.

*

After she put her empty bowl back on the table, her
wandering took her to the wall of rocks that faced the North
Sea. She carefully climbed over them, and before long, Karr
was standing next to her. "I do love the ocean so," she said.
"Grandfather and I used to sit on the rocks and watch the
waves. I shall miss that most of all, I think. Do you love the
ocean?"

"Aye." Instead of paying his full attention to her, he was more interested in looking for the hundred Viking ships that were no doubt searching for the brothers. He looked north as well, to see if the other two ships were coming back. Thankfully, he saw nothing.

"If only the seagulls dinna come inland at night to feed on our garden. I have no complaints save that one." He said nothing, so she gave up on having a conversation with him. His staying close to her didn't actually mean he favored her, for she was well aware her father asked him to protect her from Ronan. Even so, it was nice to have him near, even if it didn't mean anything.

She turned around and began to watch the crowd. For Catrina, the feast was the perfect opportunity to watch the other two brothers without them getting the wrong idea. When she spotted Hani, he was intently watching someone else. It took three times of following his gaze to see the pretty Macoran woman he was studying. The young woman glanced at Hani often too, and before long, Catrina began to smile. She stepped back over the rocks, and made her way through the people until she stood beside Hani. This time, she noticed, Karr did not follow her.

Karr was worried. It was the second time she sought Hani out, once with Kenna and now alone. Could it be that she had chosen him? Karr looked to see where Ronan was, knew he was still sitting on the walkway, and then turned back around to look across the sea. The sick feeling in his stomach would not go away. One thing was for sure. If she fancied Hani, Karr did not want to see it until he had time to come to terms with it.

*

"You find her pleasing?" Catrina asked Hani.

He was not at all embarrassed to admit it. "Aye."

"She is called Vonnie. She is a Macoran and she is unmarried."

"'Tis good to know."

"You'll not make her acquaintance standing here. Shall I take you to her?"

"I know not what to say to her."

"You will think of something." She started to tug on his sleeve, but Hani was reluctant. "A fearful Viking?" she asked.

"She shall not favor me."

Catrina folded her arms. "I disagree. I have seen the way she looks at you, and often. If she dinna find you pleasing, she would turn her eyes away."

"I have nothing to give her."

"Fearful *and* stubborn. You need not marry her this very day, but if you delay too long, she shall find another. She might even end up wed to Ronan."

Hani frowned. "*That*, I shall never allow."

"Then you best talk to her, at least. 'Tis how 'tis done in Scotland."

"Talk about what?"

Catrina threw up her hands. "I shall leave you in peace, then." She looked for the next brother to watch. She found it odd that Karr had his back to her, but it meant only that he was tired of protecting her. Next, she looked for Magnus.

*

The Brodie twins appeared to be inseparable, and Magnus stood between them, answering their many questions. Catrina slyly strolled up behind him, just to see what they were talking about.

"Truly? A whale?" Liliam asked, her eyes wide. Living even farther inland than the MacGreagors, she had never seen a whale.

"Three," Magnus proudly announced. "First, we heard what we thought was mournful singing, but then they three jumped out of the water not far from our ship."

"Were you frightened?"

"Nay," he lied. "Yet, the wave that hit us when they landed in the water nearly tipped the ship over."

"They dinna try to swallow you up?" Aerica asked. "We hear such awful stories."

"Nay, we quickly turned the ship and sailed away afore they could."

"That was wise," said Aerica while Liliam vigorously nodded.

Catrina was content. It looked as though Magnus had found favor in both their eyes, so she looked again for Karr. She meant to look for Steinn, but then she remembered he had not come. She could not help herself and this time, Karr was watching her again. When her eyes met his, the excitement she felt the first time was still there.

Karr was relieved when he discovered she was no longer with his brother. Still looking at her, he nodded toward something and waited. She followed his nod and grinned when she spotted her father sitting at one of the tables. Beside him was an older woman she did not recognize. The plot against her father seemed to be working, and she grinned at Karr a second time before she started that direction. Just as she eavesdropped on Magnus, she wove her way through the crowd until she stood behind her father.

*

The woman leaned a little closer to Stefan, "See the one with a flower in her hair?" The young woman they were talking about had pretty blonde hair.

"Aye," Stefan answered.

"She is one of mine. She is not yet old enough to marry, but it won't be long now."

"How many children do you have?"

"Eleven. 'Twould be more, but Michael passed two years hence."

"I have ten," Stefan admitted. He hadn't truly considered marrying again, but the idea of adding another eleven to the clan had its advantages. She was certainly more becoming than any other woman at the gathering, and she could hold a good conversation.

"Oh look," she said, "Laird Ronan is making his way over. You'll not let him have me, will you?"

Stefan chuckled and looked at the woman who was old enough to be Ronan's mother. "I shall guard you with my life."

"Oh good," said the widow. "Laird Limond promised none of us would be a bride this day. 'Tis why he brought only the lasses too old and too young for Ronan."

Stefan nearly laughed out loud. "How clever Laird Limond is. I must remember to comment on his good wits."

"Shall you protect me too, Father?" Catrina asked behind him.

He turned to answer, and noticed who was with her. "Nay, Karr shall do it for me."

At the same time, Ronan suddenly spotted Karr, made a hasty about face and walked away. If he noticed the laughter in the crowd, he didn't let on. He pretended to talk to someone else, and then returned to his lonely seat on the walkway.

As soon as Ronan was gone, Stefan turned to glare at his daughter. He raised an eyebrow, and the message was clear – he wanted her to go away. Catrina covered her mouth to stifle a giggle, took hold of Karr's sleeve and pulled him away. When they were lost in the crowd again, she said, "Did you see the look on my father's face?"

"Aye, he fancies her."

"It would seem so, but she has many children. I know the way my father thinks. He is thinking 'twould be good to add that many more to the clan."

"Twelve new MacGreagors if he marries her. Will he marry her?"

Catrina's smile faded. "I know not, but I cannae imagine so many more in the Castle."

"Perhaps some are already grown."

"Perhaps so. For us, 'twould be strange to have a mother other than the one we loved so very well."

"You might like her."

"Aye, but…" She suddenly felt a little sad. "Twould not be the same."

He took her elbow to keep her from getting too close to a cooking fire and stirred her away. "It could never be the same."

Catrina caught her breath. "What if she is slothful? If she is, I could end up with eleven more to care for."

"I have watched. You are very good with them. What would you do without children to care for?"

"Play. Never have I had time to play."

Karr again took her arm and pulled her out of the way so others could pass, and then guided her to a spot near a tree and out of the way. "Obbi could not keep his milk when he was a wee bairn. Our father was gone and our mother was unwell, so I…"

"You took care of him?"

"Aye, more often than not. Nikolas was always into everything, Almoor liked to tear things up and…"

"And you dinna want children either?"

"I do want them. I know of no better love in the world than when a wee one hugs my neck. I can feel it still. I cherish the softness of their skin, and the way their head fits in the curve of my neck when they fall asleep. 'Tis the only time in life I can keep them truly safe."

"You could not have been very many years when Obbi was born."

"Nine or ten, perhaps."

"'Tis very young indeed."

"'Tis why I would not make a good Viking and Grandfather knew it. I am too kindhearted."

"You said he sent you to us?"

"Aye, he said there would come a day and we would know it when we saw it. He was right, for when the King commanded we go on the next raid, we knew 'twas time to flee."

"All of you were to go?"

"Nay, only the three oldest, but the others would have gone someday too. I cared not so much for me, but I cannae…"

"You disobeyed your King?"

"Nay, I obeyed our Grandfather."

Catrina's smile for him was one of warm admiration, and it truly meant something. "'Tis good that you did."

He held her eyes with his and hoped she would know that his look meant something too. "Aye, 'tis very good that we did."

*

When Davie went inside, got a chair, brought it out and put it just a couple of feet away from Ronan, Muriel and Kenna moved closer so they could hear. Soon, Catrina, with Karr following, walked around the back of the Keep to the other side, where they could peek around the corner and listen as well.

Davie sat down and then said, "You sit alone, I see."

"Aye, there are none brave enough to approach me."

Davie turned his face away before he rolled his eyes. "I have heard that too."

Ronan accepted a bowl of chicken and vegetables one of the women brought him with one hand, and a bread bun with the other. He'd forgotten to bring out a table to set things on, so he dropped the bun in the stew, set the bowl on the floor and went back inside. To have to do it himself was exasperating, but he had not seen his guard or any member of his council for the better part of the day. Furthermore, he'd forgotten to assign a woman to care for him. He shouldn't have to – they should all feel privileged to wait on him. They always wanted to help the old Laird Macoran.

"Have you chosen a bride?" Davie asked when Ronan reappeared with a small table.

He set the table down, picked up his bowl and set the wet bun on the table. "You are well aware I prefer Catrina MacGreagor."

"Aye, but her father will not allow it. Did you not threaten to choose the daughter of Laird Brodie?"

"Laird Brodie dinna send his daughters for me to choose. I am quite put out."

"Then you dinna know?"

"Know what?"

"They are the twins walking on the beach with the Viking they call Magnus."

Ronan looked that direction and studied them. He dipped his spoon in the stew, shoved it in his mouth, chewed and swallowed. He picked up his bread and took a bite, even thought it was soggy. He watched as the barefoot twins eased up to the water's edge and then ran back when a wave rushed in. They too were irritatingly laughing. "They are bonnie lasses," he finally admitted, stuffing more bread in his mouth.

"Aye, they are. Laird Brodie had his lads say they were unsightly so no one would be tempted to marry them away. Now, he sends them for all to see."

With his mouth full, Ronan turned to Davie. He tried to understand the full meaning as he finished his bite. "Do you mean he hopes I shall choose one of his daughters?"

"'Tis what I think. The lad who brought them is Laird Brodie's son."

"His son? I see. Why does the son not bring his sisters here for my approval?"

Davie folded his arms. "Perhaps 'tis not the way 'tis done in the land of the Brodies."

"You mean I should approach them?"

Davie was pleased to have Ronan's full attention. "If you mean to marry one of them."

"Does the Viking mean to marry one of them?"

"Perhaps, but there *are* two."

Ronan grinned, "Indeed there are." He set his bowl down and stood up. When he marched down the stairs, he fully intended to greet the Brodie twins, but suddenly he remembered. Approaching one meant a promise of marriage, and he had not yet given up the idea of marrying his one true love – Catrina. As if he had forgotten something, he turned around, went right back up the steps, crossed the walkway, and went into the Keep.

*

The day was warm enough and Catrina lost interest in seeing what Ronan was up to, so she came out from around the corner of the Keep, went to Kenna and grabbed her hand. "Shall we not play in the water too? We've not done that since we were children."

Kenna giggled and gladly went with her friend, but not without looking back at Branan. The two of them were several yards away from Branan when she sighed. "Is he not the most handsome lad in all the world?"

"Which one this time?" Catrina asked.

"Branan Brodie, of course. He is soon to be the next Brodie laird."

"Kenna, think what you are doing. You cannae marry him and you know it."

"Why not?"

Catrina abruptly stopped and looked her friend in the eye. "Because your father shall forbid it and so shall his father. 'Tis impossible."

"Well…"

"You best not encourage Branan or we may very well have a war."

"But they are so friendly. Branan means us no harm, I am certain of it."

"I agree, but he is not his father. Laird Brodie is sure to hear of it and what then?"

Kenna hung her head. "I want to marry him and I think he wants the same."

"You prefer him above Grant, Donahue, Garth, *and* all the Vikings?"

"I do, I truly do."

Catrina puffed her cheeks. "Yet, there is no way the two of you can marry. You shall both find only misery when you cannae be together. Part yourself from him while there is still time."

"Time for what?" Branan asked. Kenna kept her head down and refused to look at him. When Catrina did the same, he asked, "Am I not the reason for your fretting?"

"Aye," said Kenna. At the same time, Catrina shook her head.

"Which is it?" Branan insisted.

"I best go play in the water," Catrina said. She scooted away as quickly as she could, leaving Kenna to face the consequences alone.

"Well?" he insisted.

"She fears…she says…"

"Go on, you may tell me."

"She says we must not fancy each other, for…"

"Aye, she is right."

Kenna started to turn away. "I know."

He took her arm and waited until she turned to face him. "You know not how many times I have watched you from afar."

"You have?"

"As often as I could. I have watched you grow up and wondered what miracle it would take just to talk to you.

Today, 'tis a miracle indeed, and I am not about to give you up so easily."

"But our fathers," she whispered, leaning a little closer to him.

"Aye, 'twill not be easy for either of us, but I have two sisters whom my father dearly loves. They shall speak to him in my favor. Hopefully, Laird MacGreagor shall do the same with your father."

"Are you…do you mean to marry me?"

He smiled finally, "I mean to ask for you when I can. Will you wait?"

She wanted very much to touch him, but there were far too many people around. "Aye."

"And shall you agree when I ask?"

Her impish little grin came quickly back. "Perhaps."

He rolled his eyes. "I'd sooner fight ten warriors than to await your answer."

"'Tis the MacGreagor way. You must ask, and then I shall answer."

"You are merciless, Kenna MacGreagor. Can you give me no hint?"

She suddenly put her hands on her hips, "You have been watching me?"

It made him laugh. "I wondered if you heard me. Aye, I am caught. What shall you do, throw water on me?"

"You saw even that?" She huffed, turned, and hurried to join Catrina. Once across the pile of rocks, Kenna sat beside her best friend and began to take off her shoes too.

"You look exceedingly happy?" Catrina said.

"I shall tell you all about it later."

"Tell me now," Catrina demanded.

"Very well, he means to ask for me." She saw Catrina's worried look and quickly continued, "After his sisters have convinced his father and your father has convinced mine." Kenna tossed her shoes aside and ran down the sandy beach to join the twins in their merriment.

Catrina looked for her father and found him still deep in conversation with the widow. None of the other Brodies had seen much of the ocean either, so they began to come to the beach, and some even went in the water. The North Sea was cold, but no one seemed to mind.

Branan Brodie rarely took his eyes off Kenna. Still, he didn't come across the wall of rocks and instead, stood behind it. Nearby, Karr didn't cross over either and once again scanned the water for Vikings. When Karr looked at him, Branan seemed worried. "Is it my brother that makes you fret?"

"Nay," Branan answered, "'Tis that my sisters cannae swim. I fear they shall go out too far."

"Magnus swims and is well aware the sea is mighty. He shall not let them go out too far."

"Then I am comforted," Branan confessed.

Next, a very odd thing happened and Catrina stopped walking on the beach to watch. The young Macoran woman had also come to play in the water...and with her was Hani. They stopped to talk to Karr, and when Vonnie smiled, she exposed a missing front tooth. To Catrina's amazement, Hani finally smiled too and he had two side teeth missing. Just then, a wave crashed against Catrina's legs. She let out a surprised yelp, ran up the incline, and then bent over laughing.

It wasn't long before several others joined in the fun and soon, half the people were on the beach playing. Karr found himself standing between Branan Brodie and Laird Limond.

It wasn't hard for Laird Limond to guess what Karr kept looking for. "They passed yesterday," he whispered.

"Did they? How many?"

"Eight ships fully loaded. They went south, but I suspect they shall come back once other clans run them off."

"We best stay inland for a time," said Karr. "We dinna mean to bring them down on you or the Macorans."

"I know. On the other hand, I'd give half my life to see you toss Ronan against that tree again."

Karr looked back, and spotted Ronan still sitting on the walkway beside Davie. Half the courtyard was now empty and Ronan looked just as miserable. "I wait for him to demand Catrina, but he has yet to have his say."

"Nor shall he; not with you here."

Karr smirked, "Pity, I was looking forward to fighting him."

"I hear Davie means to challenge him later."

"Does he? I shall be happy to watch that."

"Me too." Laird Limond laughed when one of the Brodie men slipped in the sand and slid into the water. Before the receding ocean could draw him out, Magnus offered his hand.

*

Tired, Catrina found a rock to sit on away from the others and in no time, Kenna joined her. Karr wasn't watching her, she noticed, but he didn't seem to be watching any other woman either.

"Have you seen the way Muriel flirts with Grant? Never have I seen such a deceitful display."

"Aye, but what do you care now?"

Kenna shrugged. "You are right, I dinna care…now."

"Then you shall be kind to Muriel?"

Kenna stiffened. "Why do you always say I am unkind?"

"Because you always are."

"She forever deserves it."

"Kenna, you have the lad you want, can you not be pleased for Grant, at least. It is easy to see he prefers her to all others."

Kenna caught her breath. "If he weds her, she shall live with us."

"And if you wed a Brodie, you shall not."

Kenna turned to stare into Catrina's eyes. "I had not thought of that."

"You have not thought of many things…not clearly, anyway."

"It seems I have not." She couldn't help herself. She looked at Branan and smiled. "Is he not the most handsome lad in the whole of the world?"

Catrina didn't think so, but she didn't say it. Instead, she watched the waves rush to shore and then recede, just as she had as a child seated beside her Grandfather. Never had she known a day without fear of the Brodies, and for the next hour, she watched members of all four clans play as if they were children who had known each other all their lives.

This day of peace and laughter, she would remember for the rest of her life.

*

For two days, Davie's sister steamed Valerian roots over her cooking fire, for she often needed a sip or two of wine and 'simples' to help her sleep at night. Therefore, she thought nothing of it when Davie asked that she make a flask of it, with a touch more simples than usual, to help him sleep.

Ronan was already beside himself with dismay over being completely ignored, particularly by the Brodies, so when Davie offered him a goblet of wine, he was happy to have it. The taste was pleasing, the contents seemed to calm his upset and when he emptied his goblet, he held it out to Davie for a refill.

Davie drank right along with him, or so Ronan thought, and before long, he felt relaxed enough to smile occasionally. "So many bonnie lasses, how shall I ever choose a wife?"

"You have decided against Catrina?" Davie asked.

Ronan snickered, "I prefer her, but if I choose her, I fear meeting the tree again."

"You are very wise, Laird Macoran."

It was the first time anyone had called him that and Ronan found it exhilarating. "I find the Brodie twins quite pleasing...quite pleasing indeed." He paused to rub his forehead and then went on. "I suppose, since Laird Brodie dinna come his...self, I am forced to go see him."

"You would risk capture and slavery?"

Ronan's mouth dropped. "Capture? Dare he capture me?"

"I know of nothing to stop him. If such were to happen, the Limonds would not risk a war to save you, and neither would the MacGreagors."

"And the Macorans?" Ronan asked.

"Without the Limonds, what are we? Certainly, we are not large enough to win against the Brodies. Alone, we are too few."

Ronan took another long drink and thought that over. "The Brodies dinna capture my lads when I sent them."

"True. What do you suppose Laird Brodie is up to?"

Ronan's eyes widened a little, but not that much. He stared at the boards in the walkway for a very long time before his eyelids began to droop. "What do *you* suppose he is up to?"

"I think he means to trap you."

"Do you? Truly?"

"I see no other reason for it. If he has you, he has us, you see."

Ronan worriedly scratched the top of his head. He could hardly keep his eyes open and he saw them, but didn't really notice the members of his council as they came up the steps. "What should I do?"

"Well, if you were no longer the Macoran laird, you would be safe."

"Safe? I...I..."

"Truly, what has it benefited you so far? You can always say you *were* a laird once, and I shall make you my fourth in command."

"You would do that for me?" Ronan asked in amazement.

"I surely would. 'Tis a place of great honor."

Ronan knew there was no such thing as a forth in command, but he was so tired the reasoning quickly escaped his mind. "Aye, honor."

"And you'd not have to fight me for it this day?"

Once more, Ronan's eyes widened a little, but they quickly went back to drooping. "I dinna want to fight, I...I favor sleeping instead."

"You may sleep as long as you like," said Davie, "once you give the Macorans the lad they truly want for their laird. They shall always honor you for it."

"Aye, honor." His head began to tilt to one side. His left eye closed and then his right.

It was too soon, so Davie grasped his shoulder and shook him. "Shall you step down, then?"

"I must, if I am to sleep."

Davie looked to the men standing behind Ronan. "Have you heard?" All three of them nodded. Two helped Ronan down the steps and took the sleeping man to his old cottage.

Enthralled, the crowd stopped what they were doing and watched in silence.

"He has stepped down," Davie announced. "I am Laird of the Macorans." His announcement was greeted with cheers and applause. "Begin the games!" he shouted.

*

Seated beside Stefan at the table, Laird Limond wrinkled his brow. "How do you suppose he managed to do that?"

"I dinna know, but I shall be forever grateful."

"As shall I. What say you we greet this new, right dead brilliant laird. 'Tis better to have a lad like that with us, than against us."

Stefan nodded, excused himself from the widow and followed Laird Limond. It wasn't long until Davie admitted the truth – the feast was Branan Brodie's idea. Once more, Branan Brodie found great favor in the eyes of Laird MacGreagor and Laird Limond. The only one still standing in the way of true peace was the old goat.

*

It was no wonder then that the happy Macorans and their guests excitedly joined in the games. The table at which Stefan and Laird Limond sat was cleared off for arm wrestling. Naturally, not one of the Scots wanted to challenge the Vikings, so the Vikings could only stand nearby and watch. The people each chose their favorite Scot, and cheered when he won or moaned when he lost. At last, and to the delight of all, Hani challenged Magnus. The people cheered, placed their wagers and stood as many as ten deep on all sides around them, with the children slipping in front of the adults to get a bird's eye view.

First, it appeared Hani would be the clear winner for he was older than Magnus, but then the arms began to tilt in Magnus' favor. Half the people applauded while the other half groaned. The arms then bent in Hani's favor, making the groans and cheers in the reverse. Both men strained, as they looked each other in the eye, daring the other to make his final move. Again, the arms tilted and it looked as though Magnus would win. Beads of sweat glistened on his brow, and he raised an eyebrow daring his brother, but Hani had seen that look before. Hani narrowed his eyes, gritted his teeth and gave it his all. Yet, Magnus held firm, even though the bulging muscles in his arm were beginning to cramp. He too gritted his teeth, gave the match his last burst of energy and laid his brother's arm flat on the table.

The crowd went wild, their shouts could be heard clear across the river and after they calmed, the brothers vowed to do it again someday. Hani was not about to let his brother beat him again.

The people tried to get Karr to challenge Hani, but Karr declined. "Twould be unfair," he claimed, "for my arms are longer." That seemed to pacify most of them. Already sore and tired, Hani was relieved.

Next came the ring toss. Short lengths of rope were tied to make the rings, while a wooden stake was pounded into the ground. It looked much easier than it was, for unless the ropes were thrown exactly so, the ring collapsed before it hit the stake. Each man had a go at it and all of them missed, until Branan Brodie gave it a try. He held the rope with both hands, keeping the circle open, and with a flick of his wrists, the rope ring exactly landed around the peg. Everyone was astounded and it took a moment, but he got the resounding applause he deserved.

Liliam whispered to Catrina, "'Tis a favorite in our clan and he nearly always wins."

"'Tis trickery of some kind," whispered her twin.

Catrina giggled. "I am convinced all lads use trickery. Do you fancy Magnus?" She looked from twin to twin, but it was Aerica, who answered.

"I find him very pleasing, but Father…"

"I know, 'tis the same for your brother."

"We mean to convince him, for Branan's sake," said Aerica.

"And not for your own?" Catrina asked.

Liliam winked, "We can but empty one heavy basket at a time."

Catrina understood completely. "So true."

They watched as three more men managed to get the ropes around the stake. Then they each took another turn. Once more, Branan's rope encircled it exactly, but only one of the other two men were successful. The two remaining waited for the crowd to finish placing their wagers, took a third turn and this time, Branan missed.

"He did it on purpose," Aerica and Liliam said at the same time.

Catrina nodded. "If he did, he is very wise."

With Ronan put away in his cottage, Catrina had no need of Karr's protection and it made her a little sad. He had no reason to watch her or even be near her now, and indeed, he was not. When she looked for him, he was talking to a Macoran. At least, it was a man and not a woman. Still, she missed seeing his glorious eyes whenever she wanted. Her sigh was heavy when she decided to ignore her disappointment and watch the archers.

The archery contests were held not far from the graveyard, where no one could be accidentally shot. The only MacGreagor participating in that challenge was Grant, and she soon lost interest. Back in the courtyard, the children were having footraces. Kenna joined Catrina, and they watched those for a while.

At last, the tired crowd began to gather near the steps of the Keep where a man climbed the steps carrying a Gemshorn made of a goat horn, and another joined him carrying a hand carved, heart shaped harp. Lastly, three singers arrived. At first, their songs were upbeat and several danced a jig to them. Some of the men clearly had partaken of a little too much wine and made the crowd laugh. Just before the guests had to leave if they intended to make it home before dark, the mood changed. The singers switched to love songs – the kind of love between a man and a woman, and then the kind of love they all shared for Scotland.

Too soon, it was time for the MacGreagors and the Brodies to gather their horses, say their goodbyes, and start back up the path toward home.

*

Silence between them was the norm, especially for those who had fallen in love. With Stefan and Hani in the lead, Branan made certain to have Kenna by his side, Magnus rode with Aerica Brodie, and Karr kept his horse even with

Catrina's. It was a good sign, Catrina thought. Grant rode beside Muriel and when they came to her father's farm, he went to the cottage to ask for her. Muriel was thrilled, and so was her father.

The time soon came for the Brodies to separate from the MacGreagors, and it was sorrowful for Kenna, Branan, Magnus, and Aerica. With a final look into the eyes of the woman he had loved for many months, Branan bravely led his people across the MacGreagor courtyard, around the wall, and down the path.

Everyone in the clan wanted to know every detail and Catrina was happy to tell them, but Kenna, she noticed, went to her cottage and closed the door. It nearly broke her heart and she was glad to know Karr would be there when she woke up. As darkness fell, she took the children inside, just as she always did, and closed her door as well.

That night, she lay awake considering all that had happened. While there were signs, Karr did not say he loved her, nor had he asked for her. Perhaps he would tomorrow or the next day, she thought. She pulled her blankets up...and closed her eyes to dream of the arms that would someday hold her.

*

Three days passed.

Karr made no sign that he intended to ask for Catrina and Branan Brodie did not come back, although Kenna often looked up the hill to see if he was watching her. If he was there, she couldn't see him.

"I am so very miserable," she confessed, on the forth morning when she made her usual visit to Catrina in the Keep.

"I know you are. Would that I could do something to ease your pain, but I cannae."

"I told Mother, but she refuses to talk to Father about Branan. You are right; we should have made a run for it."

Catrina had forgotten she said that. "Aye, but now we would only take our misery with us."

"You love Karr, do you not?"

"Aye." Catrina gathered the empty porridge bowls and began to carry them to the bucket of water. "It matters not, for he does not ask for me. He has had three days, and he looks at me. He even smiles often, but still he does not ask."

"Karr must be waiting for something, just as I must wait for something, although I cannae think what he waits for. If Branan does not do something soon, I think to stand on the wall and scream."

Catrina laughed. "May I join you?"

"Aye."

Her mother's far off voice interrupted them, "Kenna!"

Kenna tipped her head to one side. "What could she *possibly* want now? Do you suppose I shall still be able to hear her, even after I go to the Brodie village?" She didn't wait for an answer and started for the door. "'Twould be just my luck."

# CHAPTER 12

Catrina was about to finish the last of her indoor chores when her father came in and closed the door. "I wish a word with you."

"Have I done something wrong?"

"Nay, you have not." He helped himself to a goblet of ale and sat down at the table. "I have decided to take a wife."

Her mouth dropped. Slowly, she sunk into the chair beside him. "I dinna think you would. Is it the widow you spoke to at the feast?"

"Aye. I believe she is a good woman and will do well for the children."

"All one and twenty of us."

"She has but five that are yet unmarried. I am hopeful her older children will want to join our clan too."

Catrina sighed her relief. "Only five. Good. When shall you have time to marry?"

"We must finish the planting, of course, but there shall be time in a month or two."

"I see."

He took her hand in his. "Now you shall be free to marry too."

Catrina smiled. "Has he asked for me?"

"Not yet, but he shall."

"Why does he wait?"

"I dinna know, perhaps he waits until he is certain you shall not deny him. Do you love him?"

"More than I thought possible."

"More than me?"

She laid her head on her father's shoulder. "I could never love anyone more than you, but perhaps I love him just as much."

"Then I shall give my permission when he asks." He wrapped his arms around her, kissed the top of her head, and then laid his head against hers. "I am proud to call you daughter."

She wanted to say more, but Conan burst through the door with a terrified look in his eyes. "Old Blue does not wake, Father. Can you not come?"

Stefan squeezed Catrina one last time, got up, lifted his youngest son into his arms and went outside.

*

As the MacGreagor were giving Old Blue a proper dog burial, Branan sat at the table in the Brodie Keep with his father and both of his sisters. The bottom floor of the two-story Keep intentionally had no windows. The Keep was the best place to be in an attack, and allowing access through a window was too dangerous. Instead, the lighting came from a multitude of candles set on tables between jewel-encrusted golden goblets, silver pitchers, vases, and an array of other very valuable items.

Branan finished his last bite, washed it down with wine and turned to his father. "Aerica wishes to marry a MacGreagor and so do I."

It took two full days for Laird Brodie to recover from the headache his cranberry wine caused, among other problems, and even now, he wasn't sure he heard correctly. He looked from his daughter to his son and back to his daughter again. "Is this true, Aerica?"

"Aye, Father."

He again turned to his son. "Has MacGreagor put you up to this? Does he offer his daughter to you, only to form an alliance?"

"Nay, 'tis not his daughter," Branan answered.

Laird Brodie contemplated the implications. "Yet, if Aerica lives among the MacGreagors, 'tis the same as an alliance. MacGreagor knows full well I shall not attack as long as she lives there."

"I am not certain what he knows," Branan argued, "but this much I do know – your daughter wishes to marry the Viking they call Magnus."

"Has he asked for her?"

"Not yet."

"No, nor shall he ever? He fears me, as do all the clans."

Branan glanced at the hopeful look in his sister's eyes. "True, he cannae come to ask, for fear you shall sell him into slavery."

"There, you see, 'tis impossible. Likewise, Stefan MacGreagor will not allow it. He hates the sight of me. I shall leave no daughter of mine to his mercy, not while I walk the earth."

"And me?" Branan asked. "Have you not always wanted me to marry? I tell you, I shall have no other wife save Kenna MacGreagor."

Incensed and truly not yet feeling well, Laird Brodie put a hand atop his aching head. "I should not have let you take the lasses to the feast. This is my reward, I see. Choose a Limond or a Macoran, if you must marry other than a Brodie, but *not* a MacGreagor."

"Father…" Aerica started to plead.

"Look at her, Father," Branan interrupted. "If you dinna make peace with Laird MacGreagor and let her marry, she shall hate you for it."

"Make peace with him? He wishes to see me dead. I hardly think that will make her happy."

"He wishes you to end our part in the slavery. We wish it as well."

His ire was beginning to rise and his voice grew louder. "End it? There is much to gain still."

"Father, look around. How much more do we need? The clan shall never starve, even when the crops fail. We buy all that we want and we shall have need of nothing more for many years to come."

Laird Brodie slowly did as his son suggested and took a good, long look at his surroundings. As he did, Branan and his sisters quietly got up and went outside.

*

Everything had changed. One afternoon of talking instead of fighting with the Brodies brought a guarded sense of peace to the MacGreagors. Still, no one knew what the old goat would do. Therefore, Wallace and his brothers continued to take turns sitting on the wall to watch. It seemed a hopeless cause for none of them had seen so much as a hunter in days – that is, until Stefan's eldest son spotted movement on the path.

"Brodies!" Wallace shouted.

Stefan was about to go inside for the evening meal, when he stopped and went to the wall instead. "How many?"

"But one so far, and he comes quickly. 'Tis Laird Brodie."

Stefan's mouth dropped. "He comes without a guard?"

"Aye, Father. Not even his son is with him."

Inside the Castle, Kenna instantly got excited. "He has come at last," but when she heard Branan had not come, her shoulders slumped. "He has *not* come."

Even with only one Brodie spotted...so far, the people armed themselves. Yet, instead of running for safety, they gathered in front of the castle to hear firsthand what Laird Brodie had to say.

Just as Wallace announced, Laird Brodie came alone. He raced his horse around the edge of the half-finished stonewall, swung down in front of Stefan, and drew his sword. "Arm yourself, MacGreagor, I have come so that you may kill me, finally."

Stefan's expression turned from shock to rage. He started to reach for his sword, but then he thought better of it. "For the sake of your son and daughters, I shall not kill you, though killing is what you deserve."

"Then kill me. My son wishes to marry a MacGreagor and I'll not have you hating him because I yet live."

Stefan stared into the eyes of the only man in the world he truly hated. "You are asking us to live in peace with the Brodies?"

Laird Brodie slowly lowered his sword. "My son is asking it. Arm yourself and do away with me. If I am dead, he shall be free to do as he wishes, even if it means making an alliance with you...though I dread the very thought of it." He looked at all the faces watching him, and then glared at

Stefan again. "Must I cut you to tempt you to fight?" When Stefan still made no move to draw his sword, Laird Brodie shook his head in defeat and put his away. "My son demands we stop our part in the slavery."

"And shall you?" Stefan hesitantly asked.

"Is that not the only way you shall agree to the marriage?"

Secretly delighted, Stefan kept his face expressionless. "Aye, 'tis the only way."

Once more, Laird Brodie looked over the crowd, though this time he seemed more interested in the Vikings. "Which is Magnus?"

Magnus boldly stepped forward. "I am."

"My daughter fancies you. If you wish to have her, you may ask now."

Magnus didn't take his eyes off the man Aerica and her sister called the old goat. "I shall come to ask for her when the slavery has stopped, and not before."

Laird Brodie sighed. "I thought as much. You condemn me to two unhappy daughters, and one son who might soon be truly angry enough to kill me. Very well, as of this day, we shall capture lads no more." He gathered his reins and mounted his horse. "I know not which my son has chosen, but she shall be safe with us, I give you my pledge." He turned, rode his horse around the end of the wall, and raced away.

*

It took less than two days for word to spread that the Brodies had given up their evil ways. There was to be a new laird, for the old goat fully intended to step down in favor of his son. On the second day, Branan rode into the MacGreagor village and asked for Kenna. Her father was not easily persuaded, but in the end, Branan got his way and promised to return in a week's time with the Priest. Excited beyond words, Kenna and Catrina went to the Macoran village to buy linen for Kenna to wear on her wedding day.

Not completely certain they could trust the Brodies, all seven of the brothers and Stefan rode to the Brodie village so Magnus could ask for Aerica. Once the arrangement was made, Magnus promised to marry her the same day as Branan and Kenna were to be married. At last, one of the brothers had found a wife.

The work on the wall stopped. Instead, they began a new cottage for Magnus and his bride. Stefan took the time to visit his old friend, Laird Limond. Naturally, he spent time with the widow as well, and met all her children. It occurred to him, that since the priest was coming anyway, he might as well get married too. Therefore, three weddings were planned for the same day.

Hani considered it, but there was no way to build enough cottages in time. He and the Macoran woman with a missing tooth could wait.

Grant, who already had a cottage of his own, thought joining in the multiple weddings was a splendid idea, and so did Muriel. The wedding couples grew to four.

And still, Karr did not ask for Catrina.

# CHAPTER 13

He had not stopped watching her…that much she knew, but Karr made no effort to single her out, nor did he find an occasion to talk to her. As the hours passed and then the days, she found herself fearful and heartsick at times. At other times, she was furious. Worse still, Kenna looked at her with pity, her father seemed anxious for her sake, and the children were suddenly far too annoying. Everyone seemed to be watching her and finally, she had come to the end of her endurance.

Nearly in tears, she marched up the garden hill, went into the trees where no one could see, and drew her sword. She thought to ferociously drive it into the ground, but her anger had once more turned to unimaginable sorrow. It was clear he didn't want her and she was so sure he did. He gave her every indication, or so she thought. How could she have been so wrong? She hoped he had followed her and waited, but he had not. It made her even more miserable.

She desperately longed for him. Did he not long for her? Apparently not.

Catrina put her sword back in its sheath and made an important decision. Work was always the way to keep her mind off her troubles, and there was plenty of planting to do. That was it – she would completely ignore him, and work until the hurt finally went away.

Thus, Catrina stopped looking at him and Karr found it confusing. He had done something wrong, but he could not guess what. A vigilant man where she was concerned, he saw her begin to work in the garden soon after the morning meal. From a bag, she began to sow seeds into the ground and then cover them with dirt. It was grueling work and he saw her stop only once to take a sip of water in the unusually warm day.

He helped put up the walls to Magnus' new cottage. The morning passed to afternoon and then to the beginning of evening, and although he glanced at her often, he did not continually watch her, If he had, he would have noticed something was wrong long before he did. When at last he did notice, he dropped the rock he carried, and took off running.

Catrina was standing up, but she had completely stopped moving. Her hand was still in the bag of seeds, her eyes were closed and she had begun to sway by the time Karr lifted one of her arms over his head and then lifted her up. The bag of seeds fell to the ground and she awoke with a start. "What is it?"

He put his cheek next to hers and as he suspected, she was feverish. Not long after, Stefan arrived. "She is too hot," Karr whispered.

"Have I done something wrong, Father?" she asked.

"Nay, sweetheart," Stefan answered. Before he could suggest it, Karr carried her down the hill, across the courtyard, and into the water. He waded far enough out for the water to cover most of her body, and then he began to slowly turn, letting the water wash over her. "Sleep, Catrina. I shall not let you fall."

She tried to smile. "I have never known the water to be so warm." She laid her head against his arm, and she wanted to sleep, but she was in his strong arms finally and she didn't want to waste the moment. Catrina should not have, for it was not proper, but she desperately needed to know. "Why have you not asked for me?"

"Did you not say you wanted no more children to care for? If we marry, 'tis a promise I cannae make."

Catrina bit her lower lip. "I did say that."

"Aye, you did. Have you changed your mind?"

She closed her eyes and let the water rush over her a little while longer. "I *have* changed my mind."

Karr stopped turning and took a relieved breath. When she reached up to touch his face, he lifted her out of the water so she could wrap her arms around his neck, and then he gently kissed her lips. "I love you even more than my father loved my mother."

She laid her head on his shoulder and closed her eyes. "Yours are the arms I felt, even before you came."

"I dreamed of you too."

This time when he kissed her, her heart filled with a joy she could not contain. At last, she understood. Having his children was not the same. He was the man she waited for, and she knew he was filled with goodness and kindness just as she was. He made no threats, he promised nothing and he was not stupid.

It was a perfect match.


~ the end~

# MORE MARTI TALBOTT BOOKS

Read Marti's historical novels in chronological order:

**The Viking Series:**

The Viking

The Viking's Daughter

The Viking's Son

(There is a gap of about 500 years and then the MacGreagor Clan stories continue.)

**Marti Talbott's Highlander Series:**

The Highlander Omnibus (Books 1-3)

Marti Talbott's Highlander Series 1

Marti Talbott's Highlander Series 2

Marti Talbott's Highlander Series 3

Marti Talbott's Highlander Series 4

Marti Talbott's Highlander Series 5

Betrothed, Book 6

The Golden Sword, Book 7

Abducted, Book 8

A Time of Madness, Book 9

Triplets, Book 10

Secrets, Book 11

Choices, Book 12

Ill-Fated Love Book 13

The Other Side of the River, Book 14

(Again, there is a 500 year gap before the MacGreagor stories continue.)

**Marblestone Mansion,** (Scandalous Duchess Series)
The Marblestone Mansion Omnibus (Books 1-3)
Marblestone Mansion, (Scandalous Duchess Series)  Book 1
Marblestone Mansion, (Scandalous Duchess Series)  Book 2
Marblestone Mansion, (Scandalous Duchess Series)  Book 3
Marblestone Mansion, (Scandalous Duchess Series)  Book 4
Marblestone Mansion, (Scandalous Duchess Series)  Book 5
Marblestone Mansion, (Scandalous Duchess Series)  Book 6
Marblestone Mansion, (Scandalous Duchess Series)  Book 7
Marblestone Mansion, (Scandalous Duchess Series)  Book 8
Marblestone Mansion, (Scandalous Duchess Series)  Book 9
Marblestone Mansion, (Scandalous Duchess Series)  Book 10

**Lost MacGreagor Stories,** will fill in the gap between the Highlanders and Marblestone.
Beloved Ruins
Beloved Lies

**Other Marti Talbott books.**
**The Jackie Harlan Mysteries**
Seattle Quake 9.2, Book 1
Missing Heiress Book 2
Greed and a Mistress, Book 3

**The Carson Series**

The Promise, Book 1

Broken Pledge, Book 2

**Leanna**   A short story

Keep informed about new book releases and talk to Marti on Facebook at:

https://www.facebook.com/marti.talbott

Sign up to be notified when new books are published at:

http://www.martitalbott.com

Made in the USA
Lexington, KY
03 April 2016